Somehow, Some Way

Also from Jennifer Probst

The Billionaire Builders
Everywhere and Every Way
Any Time, Any Place
All Or Nothing At All

Searching for Series:
Searching for Someday
Searching for Perfect
Searching for Beautiful
Searching for Always
Searching for You

The Marriage to a Billionaire series:
The Marriage Bargain
The Marriage Trap
The Marriage Mistake
The Marriage Merger
The Books of Spells

Executive Seduction

All the Way

The Sex on the Beach Series:
Beyond Me
Chasing Me

The Hot in the Hamptons Series:
Summer Sins

The Steele Brother Series:
Catch Me
Play Me
Dare Me
Beg Me

Dante's Fire

Somehow, Some Way

A Billionaire Builders Novella

By Jennifer Probst

1001 Dark Nights

EVIL EYE
CONCEPTS

Somehow, Some Way
A Billionaire Builders Novella
By Jennifer Probst

1001 Dark Nights

Copyright 2017 Triple J Publishing Inc
ISBN: 978-1-945920-35-6

Foreword: Copyright 2014 M. J. Rose

Published by Evil Eye Concepts, Incorporated

Acknowledgments from the Author

Huge thanks, kudos, and squishy hugs to the fabulous Liz Berry and MJ Rose. This 1001 Dark Nights family you've built is so much better than the mob. And much safer too. I'm so honored to be part of this.

Thanks to Kim Guidroz for the wonderful edits and feedback. Thanks to Jillian Stein for being one of the best bloggers in the entire planet and integral to this team.

I cannot tell you how many more fabulous authors I got hooked on by reading these books. You've all done a service to readers who love a great love story. That is your greatest success of all.

Dedication

Anyone who's read my books know I love to write about strong women.

I'd like to dedicate this book to Rosemary Conlon – my godmother and beloved Aunt, who taught me about all the fabulous things in life. Thanks for being an important part of my life and always believing in me. I love you.

Sign up for the 1001 Dark Nights Newsletter
and be entered to win a Tiffany Key necklace.

There's a contest every month!

Go to www.1001DarkNights.com to subscribe.

As a bonus, all subscribers will receive a free
1001 Dark Nights story
The First Night
by Lexi Blake & M.J. Rose

One Thousand and One Dark Nights

Once upon a time, in the future…

*I was a student fascinated with stories and learning.
I studied philosophy, poetry, history, the occult, and
the art and science of love and magic. I had a vast
library at my father's home and collected thousands
of volumes of fantastic tales.*

*I learned all about ancient races and bygone
times. About myths and legends and dreams of all
people through the millennium. And the more I read
the stronger my imagination grew until I discovered
that I was able to travel into the stories… to actually
become part of them.*

*I wish I could say that I listened to my teacher
and respected my gift, as I ought to have. If I had, I
would not be telling you this tale now.
But I was foolhardy and confused, showing off
with bravery.*

*One afternoon, curious about the myth of the
Arabian Nights, I traveled back to ancient Persia to
see for myself if it was true that every day Shahryar
(Persian: شهریار, "king") married a new virgin, and then
sent yesterday's wife to be beheaded. It was written
and I had read, that by the time he met Scheherazade,
the vizier's daughter, he'd killed one thousand
women.*

Something went wrong with my efforts. I arrived in the midst of the story and somehow exchanged places with Scheherazade – a phenomena that had never occurred before and that still to this day, I cannot explain.

Now I am trapped in that ancient past. I have taken on Scheherazade's life and the only way I can protect myself and stay alive is to do what she did to protect herself and stay alive.

Every night the King calls for me and listens as I spin tales. And when the evening ends and dawn breaks, I stop at a point that leaves him breathless and yearning for more. And so the King spares my life for one more day, so that he might hear the rest of my dark tale.

As soon as I finish a story... I begin a new one... like the one that you, dear reader, have before you now.

Chapter One

"It's not the beauty of a building you should look at; it's the construction of the foundation that will stand the test of time."—*David Allan Coe*

Her gaze ate up the gorgeous build before her. Oh, this one was hot. Her hands ached to touch, stroke, enjoy. Immerse herself in the dirty, sweaty actions that would fulfill them both.

No.

She paused, pressing a hand to her mouth. What was wrong with her? Why was she always attracted to the ones needing so much damn work? It was like she craved to be the savior, restoring all the broken parts to achieve wholeness and beauty. How many times had she been bitterly disappointed by the result? By her investment in time and energy that never seemed to be enough?

Could she stand to take another risk?

Charlotte Grayson squeezed her eyes shut and struggled with the raw lust shooting through her body, competing with her sensible, overworked brain that screamed for her to walk away.

"Earth to Charlie."

Her lids flew open. And once again, she succumbed to bad-boy charm and the lure of the challenge. "I want him."

Her contact lifted a brow. Gage was a bit cutthroat in business but held a soft spot for her. No one ever took him as a serious competitor. His uniform was a backward red baseball cap, jeans with holes in the knees that weren't fashionable, nerdy white sneakers, and a T-shirt that declared BEER IS GOOD. With his nondescript features, unshaven jaw, and casual attitude, he looked like he'd rather be smoking weed in the garage than flipping dilapidated properties for a profit. Another reason Charlie liked him. People had been misjudging her forever, and it was nice to meet another of her kind. "How come you always call them he?" he asked curiously, scratching his head.

She shrugged. "Probably my warped way of controlling men?" she suggested. "I get to do what I want, when I want. Give them a makeover. Be their one and only for a while." She shot him a mischievous grin. "And I also get to be the one to break up with them. Kind of poetic, right?"

"Kind of weird, but you've always been a bit quirky." Gage grinned back and they both surveyed the house. "We'll need to close quick. I had a few other contacts interested but I showed this to you first."

"Always knew you had a crush on me, Gage." She batted her lashes, confident their relationship was on solid ground from any sexual minefields. His partner, Tom, would kick her ass if she tried to lure Gage to the land of women.

He snorted. "I just knew you'd be loony enough to grab it."

The sweet sizzle of foreplay flowed rich in her veins. The house was a horror show. From the sagging porch, broken shingles, cracked windows, and weed-clogged lot, it was tucked down the back end of a street in a crappy neighborhood. Most flippers would stay far away, but they didn't have her vision. Already, her hands itched to begin to restore and see how she could transform the brokenness into something truly beautiful.

Finally, she had her own project. She'd been saving money furiously in the past year for this very moment. Her first house to renovate on her own. It was a heady thrill that rivaled the feel of drinking too much champagne.

"Wait till you see him when I'm done."

He glanced around the deserted neighborhood. "Trapps isn't the best area. Don't make me regret selling you this by working out here alone."

She sniffed. "I'm not stupid, Gage."

"I know. They had a drug bust a few blocks over last week. Just want you to be careful."

"Land is getting scarce in Harrington, though. I like the idea of working within the outskirts of town before some billionaire beats me to it. There's tons of investors looking to scoop up property. I intend to be one of the first they buy."

His brown eyes lit with admiration. "You're too cool for a girl, Charlie."

She sighed. "I know. It's hard to find friends who want to spend their spare time ripping apart houses instead of doing their nails."

"Still at Pierce Brothers?" he asked.

"Yeah. I really like it." Her job at the customized builders had morphed to full time, and she was finally beginning to carve out a name for herself. This project would give her the extra push for her career. If she did this right, and Pierce approved, she'd get more opportunities, and maybe even a raise.

"Good. Maybe they'll help you out with this atrocity." He winked, taking the sting from his words, and pivoted on his sneakered heel. "Let's go sign some paperwork so I can get home in time for dinner. Tom's making Irish stew."

Her stomach grumbled on cue. Damn, she was always forgetting to eat. "How'd you get so lucky to hook up with a chef?"

"I date actual people. Not houses who are pretend boyfriends."

She laughed, not taking offense.

After all, he was right. Not that she had any issues with real men. She even liked sex, when she was able to tear her gaze away from a renovation long enough to satisfy her physical needs. The main problem was the quality, not quantity. She'd never had a problem securing dates, compliments, or interest from the opposite sex. It was keeping her attention that was the issue. Most men she dated seemed…flat. Once any physical chemistry faded, she was left with an itch to move on. Of course, men seemed to love the whole challenge aspect and immediately gave chase until she ended up having to either lie to spare their feelings, or hand out brutal honesty that sucked. She hated hurting people. Hell, she didn't even know what she wanted in a man anymore, so maybe that's why they got confused. She wouldn't mind a steady relationship, as long as it wasn't serious. Or boring. Or demanding. Or draining.

Ah, hell, it was so much easier to stick with houses.

She followed Gage back to the office, pushing away her thoughts, and concentrated on the new boy toy that would soon be all hers.

Chapter Two

"You need a plan to build a house. To build a life, it is even more important to have a plan or goal."—Zig Ziglar

Brady Heart crossed his arms in front of his chest and stared at the woman seated in his office. Already, prickles of heat sizzled on his skin like a heat rash. Good thing he knew it wasn't an allergy. He'd dealt with this before and knew the official term for his outbreak.

Irritation.

This seemed to be the normal reaction when he was in the vicinity of one single female.

Charlotte Grayson.

His penetrating look usually did the trick in quelling any type of opposition. He knew the art of silence and used it accordingly. Most women her age would be squirming in their seat and trying desperately to come up with clever quips to soothe his temper.

Not her. Even worse, she didn't even look like she was trying to challenge him back. She just looked...bored. Which pissed him off to no end.

Because when he was around her, he was everything *but* bored.

He clamped down the urge to scratch his skin, which was suddenly stretched too tight over his body. Especially in certain areas of his anatomy that seemed to gleefully rise to the occasion whenever Ms. Grayson was around.

"I told you before when I drafted the plans, I'm not going to change them again. Maybe you need to learn how to make up your mind so your renovations don't become a mismatched puzzle. I prefer organization and planning when I work closely with someone." His tone was mild, with a touch of disapproval—the perfect balance when dealing with stubborn coworkers who carried around a cloud of chaos like Pig Pen carried a cloud of dust.

Except she didn't look impressed. Dressed in another ridiculous outfit that made her look like a high schooler, she faced him with a mulish expression. For God's sake, hadn't anyone taught her to dress professionally? Her leggings were a wild mix of painted pinks, yellows, and blues, shades that startled an onlooker with all those bright colors hitting at once. Her T-shirt was basic, except for the way it pulled tight across her impressive chest and scrolled ANGEL in pink script. It was the type of outfit that emphasized the ripe curves held in a petite frame. Her sneakers were a metallic shade of silver that looked like a disco ball when she walked.

It wasn't just her clothes, either. Her hair was pin straight, with shaggy bangs. The strands weren't just blonde but a combination of cedar, honeycomb, and timber, all shaded together. Her hazel eyes were big—too big for her heart-shaped face—and framed by thick lashes. Her nose was pert, and her lips were perfectly formed. She rarely wore makeup, but liked to apply a glossy balm so her mouth resembled a juicy, shiny apple. Not Red Delicious. More like McIntosh, that held a nice pink color.

WTF?

Why the hell was he thinking of fruit and her mouth? She drove him nuts and was everything he wasn't attracted to in a woman. Including her sassy attitude. Like now.

"I think it's a shame you haven't been taught to be flexible," she retorted. Her purple nails flashed in the air. "Sometimes, creativity is more important than coloring within the lines. The house warrants our very best. I apologize if you need to redraft the plans again, but isn't that your job?"

Oh, she liked to push him. He got along with everyone else at Pierce Brothers, but as soon as they hired Charlie, he knew she'd be a challenge. What surprised him the most was her confidence. She seemed to have the ability to make him feel judged, even after years of experience in being an architect. The worst part?

He sensed she found him lacking.

"And I thought your job was to settle on a plan for renovation after carefully sifting through each option. Not to play with experimentation on my time." He kept his voice cool and impersonal, though temper heated his blood. How many times had he imagined shutting her up with his mouth over hers? He chalked it up to being sexually frustrated along with primitive emotions enclosed in a tiny workspace. Emotions that included anger and irritation logically extended to sexual attraction. He'd learned early on that being impulsive only led to disaster. He might be physically attracted to her for some strange reason, but they'd be a complete wreck after a few hours together. There was one thing he avoided at all costs in his personal relationships.

Mess.

"I did. But you kept pushing me to your timetable and now I need to redesign it." She raised one brow in pure challenge. "Would you rather our work be good? Or great?"

"My work is great," he fired back. "But you need to stop acting like Picasso with these renovations so we don't get backed up. Did you secure permission from Tristan to change the plans again?"

"Yes. He agreed." She paused. Her voice came out grudgingly. "But he said the final decision was yours."

A smug grin curved his lips. Oh, she hated having to ask him for things. He knew she considered him an uptight control freak. Maybe he was. But she needed to hone her creative outbursts and passion for ripping up houses on impulse without a solid architectural plan first.

"Hmm, funny, I didn't hear you ask me anything. Seemed more like a demand to me."

He gave her credit. She still didn't crack, but her eyes gleamed with a spark of temper that intrigued him. Why was it so much fun to rile her up? Because she seemed to dismiss him so easily in the office? Was it his ego or something more?

"I'm asking you to redo the plans because it's the right thing to do." Her tone was patient, as if trying to explain to a toddler. "It took me longer than I expected to get the right vision. I apologize if my request is causing a problem in your extremely busy schedule."

Only this woman could make an apology sound like a backhanded insult. He leaned back in the chair and studied her for a few moments in silence. As usual, she was comfortable enough in her skin to sit still and wait him out. He clicked on his keyboard and brought up his calendar to check the rest of his afternoon.

"Fine. I'll come out and see the property with you."

Her hazel eyes widened slightly. "Oh, no need. I have the photos in the office."

She seemed a bit too hasty to keep her distance. Another wave of irritation hit. She didn't act like this with the other men. Hell, he'd seen her laughing and joking with Dalton, Tristan, and Cal. It was only when he was around that she stiffened up and tried to avoid him. "I work more effectively when I can walk the site," he said. "We can head out now. I'll drive." Without another word, he stood up and straightened his tie. "Unless you don't have time in your busy schedule?"

She tightened her lips and rose. The word ANGEL sparkled with tiny pink sequins, emphasizing the lush curves of her breasts. The ultimate contradiction. Did she expect to retain the crew's respect when she worked at a site dressed in such an outfit? Not that he'd seen her in action. Only flitting in and out of the office, driving him mad with changing her design and treating him like an afterthought rather than the man who made it all happen for her. If she believed life was about impulse, fun, and following her muse, she should never have gotten into the design business. Without structure and a solid foundation—the actual plans that building and renovation revolved around—there was chaos.

Brady despised chaos.

Her tone was sugary sweet when she spoke. "I'm always up for a fun road trip. Lead the way."

He did.

* * * *

Charlie tried not to fidget in the expensive leather seat of his Mercedes-Benz. How much had this car cost him? It looked like a pilot's cockpit, with buttons, gadgets, and a big, shiny computer screen. He probably could've gotten a better deal with an American carmaker. On a holiday weekend. With a leftover model instead of the must-have newest one. Such a waste of money.

She bet he didn't care. The architect didn't seem to mind paying for luxuries if it made his life easier and more manageable. She'd pegged him the first moment they met, when his nose wrinkled and his gaze swept over her clothes, finding her lacking. The man wore a classic suit, like he was running for Congress rather than dealing with architectural plans. Always polished, groomed, with manicured fingers and a smoky, gravelly voice. It was funny because Tristan Pierce dressed like Bond himself, but never seemed to judge her wardrobe, occasional bawdy jokes, or tendency to work in disorganized chaos. He'd welcomed her to Pierce Brothers with an open mind, and when he saw her work on the first few jobs, he quickly doubled her workload. He also didn't hover or second-guess her instincts. He allowed her to lead on some jobs and told her he was impressed. He didn't care how she did her job as long as she was successful.

Not Brady.

He liked surface image. Polished women, with graceful manners. Word spread quickly around the office he only dated women who were soft spoken, well mannered, and let him lead in every way. The thought made Charlie shiver with loathing. She couldn't imagine giving her freedom over to a man just for his ego. Guess the man had no self-confidence. That would be the only reason he'd want to date a doormat or robotic Stepford Barbie.

Not that she cared.

She'd dealt with all types in the renovation business and usually could handle herself well. Too bad his lousy personality was hidden behind his looks. There was one thing she was forced to admit.

The man was hot.

Super hot. Sexy hot. Though his name was pure English, he looked all Latino, with gorgeous brown skin, sooty dark eyes, and inky, glossy, thick hair holding subtle shades of blue. One rebellious wave always fell loose over his forehead, giving just a touch of the disheveled look. His nose was a sharp blade that dominated his face. His lips were full and defined, with a slight curl to the bottom like he held a perpetual smirk. His body was hard and tight, and though he was average height, he used every one of those muscles to emanate a lean power that popped from his aura.

When he shook her hand for the first time, her skin had literally prickled with awareness. He was…intense. Thank God he wasn't her type, and she had little use for a chauvinistic male with an inflated ego.

No, thanks.

She remembered the exact moment she realized he wouldn't be the warm and fuzzy type. His judgy gaze traveled over her figure with dismissal; his mouth firmed into a thin line of disapproval, and he'd actually questioned Tristan if they really needed another employee to handle renovations.

It had taken all of her discipline not to give him the tongue lashing he deserved. He was a jerk and just plain rude. Sure, her clothes weren't conservative or polished. Yes, she looked super young and inexperienced. She might not talk like a Harvard graduate, but he didn't know her and yet he leapt to conclusions. Another trait she despised. She'd stood there, feeling a bit awkward, and Tristan had laughed and smoothly launched into a positive spiel about how much she'd help them out and how talented she was. Instead of apologizing or softening, Brady had just nodded, given her a clipped "Welcome to the team", and marched away like she wasn't worth another word.

After that, Charlie had declared a silent war on the architect. She went out of her way to make his life miserable. Oh, she wasn't proud of stooping to the level of petty vengeance, but she craved getting some kind of reaction from him. Since he'd rarely shown anger, interest, or respect, she figured she'd stick to the one she seemed to master.

Irritation.

The Mercedes purred low and sleek, like a graceful cougar. She tried to hold her tongue, but as usual, lost the battle. "How much did this car cost?"

He shot her a look, arching his brow. "A lot. Don't you think your question is a bit impolite?"

She gave a snort. Even his words were all proper. "Why is everyone so uptight about talking money?"

"It's a sensitive subject. Like politics. And sex."

Was that a deliberate pause or her imagination? The word fell from his lips like a crudely uttered curse. He seemed a bit shocked he'd uttered such a statement. Seems Brady didn't like to say the word aloud. Amusement flickered. She bet he'd be way too polite in the bedroom. Probably asked nicely for everything from start to finish, like a business dinner instead of a dirty roll in the hay. She liked a man who took what he wanted in private and seduced her into saying yes to everything. Politically incorrect, but she couldn't help what turned her on. She reached for her water bottle to take a sip and concentrated on the conversation. "If people were more honest, less miscommunication would occur."

"My car cost me $70,000."

The liquid slid down the wrong pipe and she fell into a coughing fit. He handed her a napkin, that faint disapproval flickering in his sooty eyes. He was probably terrified she'd drool on the leather. "Are you nuts?" she asked. Her voice sounded a tad shrill as she dabbed at the tears. "My truck cost ten thousand and it runs like a workhorse." It was a washed-out red with a kick-ass engine, and she loved it with a passion.

His nose wrinkled. "I've seen your truck. It's loud and obnoxious. Also ugly."

"But I got it for a steal," she retorted. "I could buy two houses with what you spent to drive around in luxury. Does sitting on a cushy car seat mean that much to you?"

"Actually, it does, especially when they're heated with an option for massage. And that is exactly why people don't talk about money."

She opened her mouth, then snapped it shut. "Sorry. Guess I'm a bit frugal."

"Some would say cheap." He flicked her a glance laced with suspicion. "Are you the one who spearheaded the movement to stop the pastries at morning meetings?"

She puffed up with pride. "Yes, I told Sydney by switching to bagels instead of those tiny overpriced sweets, you'd save money."

He groaned. "I loved those damn pastries. I looked forward to them."

She shrugged. "I just increased your bottom line."

"Fine. I'll pay for them out of my own pocket. Satisfied?"

She smothered a laugh. Questions whirled in her brain regarding how he fit in with the Pierce brothers. He was the only one who wasn't technically family. How did he get to be a partner? She'd watched him among the brothers, and he was treated like one of them—not an outsider. Pushing the impulse to blurt out a bunch of questions he'd refuse to answer anyway, she stuck to neutral topics. "Have you always wanted to be an architect?"

"Yes."

That was it? Someone needed to give him a class on how to carry on a conversation. "Cool beans." Forget it. She sure as hell wasn't going to search for safe topics to have a boring one-way conversation. She turned to the window and began to play her favorite game. Pick a house, imagine who lived there, and renovate to an imaginary world that perfectly fit her imaginary family. She'd spent hours driving around neighborhoods with her mother, peeking into windows at night, spinning tales of the families who lived behind the walls. If she had been a decent writer, maybe she could've been an author, but writing a business letter was enough for her. She liked anything that involved hands-on work that built something.

He made a grunt beside her. His next question was a bit reluctant, but she gave him credit for trying. "How did you get into home renovation?"

"I hate waste."

He lifted a brow. "Care to expound?"

"Like you?"

He stiffened, seeming a bit awkward, and she took pity on him. "I like the idea of using what's there already to make it better. People are obsessed with new. New clothes, cars, jewelry, houses. I look at the constant upgrades this world is obsessed with and it makes me sad. They're missing the potential of transforming ordinary into the extraordinary by making a few changes in what they have already. We've become a throw-away society and it pisses me off. So, yeah, to answer your question, when my friend told me she wanted the new Barbie dream house 'cause hers was old, I took it apart, renovated it, and she loved it all over again. Made me feel good. Here's the turnoff."

The car took the turn with competent ease. He shot her a strange look, as if she'd managed to surprise him, but he didn't respond and she shrugged the whole thing off. The rich scent of his cologne, a delicious mix of clove and musk, drifted to her nostrils. Probably cost a fortune. She'd always been an Old Spice type of girl.

He pulled up to the curb and cut the engine. The latest project for Pierce Brothers was a Tudor build that looked graceful from the front, but when they got inside, it was as if a puzzle had been mismatched and held together by old glue. The rooms had no flow and were individually contained in tight spaces rather than the open floor plan most customers coveted. She headed into the living room and pointed to the staircase that had been stuck in the back corner of a room solely meant for comfort and entertaining.

"Either the builder or the architect should have been jailed for this atrocity," Brady stated, his gaze registering the fireplace squooshed next to the stairs and a built-in cabinet in dull oak that had no function other than to visually assault. She laughed, already itching to transform the room into a cozy haven meant for a future family she'd never meet.

"Since we can't take them to court, let's fix it," she said.

"I already did. I gave you perfect plans already. Why do you want to change them?"

One thing she'd never fault him for was his work. His designs and outlook of a building were an art. She knew from working with other architects who were only able to see the technical aspects rather than the creative design that it limited options. Brady wasn't afraid to stretch out of his comfort zone. But he was still stubborn as hell about changing what was initially drafted. "There was nothing wrong with them. I've just come up with a better plan. If you can make it work."

"I can make anything work." His clean-shaven jaw clenched with the verbal challenge. "You have to convince me if it's worth it."

She rocked back on her silver sneakers and pointed to the ridiculous staircase. "Our first plan kept the staircase, removed the built-in, and destroyed the fireplace. Yes, it works functionally and visually, but I'd rather block off the staircase here, and extend it to the back of the room by the front door." She walked backward, her arm extended as she made sweeps in the open air. "We keep the built-in and have Dalton finish it in a rich mahogany. We keep the fireplace, restore the natural brick, and gain all this excess space that can be used as a full living room."

He tapped his finger against those carved lips, his dark brows drawn in concentration. He took a while to study the layout, examining the staircase with an intensity that intrigued her. Could he possibly have a sliver of passion buried beneath all those stringent rules and barriers?

"It's doable. But extra work with no solid purpose. It can work just as well if we keep the staircase as is."

"There's purpose. I'll have this open area where the stairs were to break through this wall and combine the dining room so we have one giant space. Come with me." She led him back to the front door and regarded the layout. "It makes no sense to have a back entrance to the upstairs and leave all this extra space open with no function. It also changes the appearance when you first walk through the door. There's no structure."

"Why now instead of when we met for the original design?" he challenged. "Sometimes if you make a mistake, you need to commit."

"Why?"

He stared at her. "What do you mean? To learn a lesson. To build discipline. To respect your coworkers. You can't go through life with a long line of unfinished products or half-assed work just because you can."

Oh, he was so uptight she wondered if he'd ever gone commando or skinny dipped or eaten ice cream in bed just for fun. "Actually, you can," she shot back. "Life isn't about putting your head down like a good little soldier and following the rules. It's about changing your mind, and making a mess, and surrendering to the moment when creativity strikes. I didn't see it before. Now, I do. The real question is do you walk away knowing it could have been better but you just didn't want to admit you were wrong the first time? Haven't you ever been wrong, Brady?"

A muscle worked in his jaw. "Of course. Everyone makes mistakes."

She tilted her head and studied him. "I know. But does everyone forgive themselves for making mistakes? I do. I want to fix it. Do you?"

His gaze met hers, and an odd heat simmered between them. "How old are you?" he demanded.

She stuck her chin in the air. "Twenty-five."

His lips twisted in a mockery of a smile. "I'm thirty-five. I've built my reputation on quality work and consistence. You want me to fix the house to suit your new vision? Fine. I can do that. But don't think making excuses to rationalize an error makes you some free-spirited, impulsive artist who knows more about life than I do."

Her mouth dropped open.

He spun on his polished heel and walked to the door. "By the way, I forgive you."

"Forgive me?" she managed to squeak out. Her vision blurred to a pale red. She'd always wondered if that cliché was true. "For what?"

"Making a mistake. I have to get back to the office. I'll have your new plans drawn up by end of day."

He disappeared through the door before she could launch herself after him and... Well, she wasn't sure what, but shaking that arrogant, cool exterior off his gorgeous face would be her first priority.

After a few moments of simmering, she stomped out, got in the car, and refused to talk to him for the rest of the drive back.

He was such an asshole.

* * * *

He was such an asshole.

Brady snuck a glance at her profile. Weak rays of sun streamed over her face, highlighting the smooth, soft skin of her cheek. An aura of steam hung over her head like a storm cloud brewing. Her gaze was trained out the window, arms clasped tight around her body, stretching the soft cotton over the lush curve of her breasts. Immediately his dick stirred to life. If he stopped the car, yanked her into his arms, and kissed her, would he finally figure out what made him so attracted to her?

He'd been hot for women before. He rarely leapt when a well-laid plan for seduction always worked better. He actually liked the foreplay and tension that flickered to a brilliant, white-hot flame. Enjoyed the play of banter and dialogue, of knowing what was to unfold between them, of the endless possibilities.

Unfortunately, he'd been wrong too many times before and he'd turned a tad cynical. Sure, he'd had some long-term relationships he'd hoped would become permanent, and many women had actually shared his same goals. Settle down to raise a family. Let him be the breadwinner and shoulder the financial responsibilities. He'd watched his father take care of his family, and now his two sisters had settled into domestic bliss. He refused to apologize for knowing who he was and what he wanted out of life. Yet each time he thought of making a permanent commitment, his soul balked. There was a restlessness inside him that never seemed to calm, and damned if he'd marry without being all in.

He knew all of his requirements, his fantasies, his needs, and his wants. When *the one* burst into his life, his heart and gut would sense his partner and everything would click into place.

Right now, he only knew one thing.

His soul mate was *not* Charlotte Grayson.

But he wanted her.

He cut her another glance, brooding over his assholery back in the house. Why did she always ignite his temper? The way she passionately pleaded a case, painting herself as a figure who raced through life grabbing every opportunity and following every impulse, while she mocked him for the very thing that brought him success.

Order. Knowledge. Control.

Probably the ten-year difference. She was a baby. She'd probably lived a pampered life, secure in her parents' house with her parents' money. She'd graduated from a proper college and decided to have some fun with rehab. Oh, she was good at her job, but this wasn't permanent for her. She had an itch to scratch, and he felt he needed to protect Pierce Brothers if she decided to go out on her own and steal any of their clients.

She couldn't do anything now, but he suspected once she found the next yellow brick road to follow, she'd be off to discover a brand new Oz. The last thing he needed in his life was a flighty woman.

But he wanted her.

He shifted in his seat, cursing under his breath. So stupid. He just needed to get over it because he sure as hell wasn't making a move. She'd probably spit in his face and sue him.

Charlotte Grayson would be shocked at some of the things he wanted to do to her. She called herself a free spirit, but he bet she'd be the type of lover to fight him on every move, questioning, pushing, until the entire episode became too complicated to be any fun.

No thanks.

He'd stick with the plan that had been working well between them. Keep his distance and limit his interaction with her. It gave him a better opportunity to be less of a dick. She didn't deserve to be insulted.

He pulled up to Pierce Brothers and cut the engine. "Charlotte, I apologize. I—"

"Don't call me that. I hate it."

"Fine. Let me explain—"

"No need to explain. I get it." She turned to him and those stunning hazel eyes regarded him with a spark of temper. "You haven't liked me from day one. Let's just agree to be polite at work and not pretend we'll ever be more than what we are—coworkers forced to share the same space."

A sting of shame hit him. "Listen, I—"

"I'll make sure from now on I get the plans right the first time so we have no further issues. Thanks for the cushy ride."

She jumped out of the car and didn't look back as she entered the office. Brady smothered a groan, rubbing his temples. Dammit, he hadn't meant to hurt her feelings. She churned him up inside and he couldn't figure out why.

Maybe it was better this way. He only worked with her on a limited basis, and it shouldn't be hard to keep his distance. He'd deliver her plans when she asked and schedule walk-throughs with Tristan so they didn't have to be alone again.

It was for the best.

Chapter Three

"Regard it as just as desirable to build a chicken house as to build a cathedral."—Frank Lloyd Wright

Charlie climbed up the broken steps, juggling the mass of supplies in her hands, and walked into the house. The scent of rotted wood and dust filled the air. Her ears strained with the sound of screaming silence. There was something so sad about an empty house. It cried of lost memories and loneliness.

She intended to fix it.

Dropping her toolbox, she grabbed her notebook and began taking inventory of the main things she wanted to accomplish. Finally, she had her own project to dive into. Her heart slammed against her ribs in excitement and anticipation. The dumpster was coming this week, but so far, she had been unable to book any extra help. Besides the expense, schedules for all her contacts were filled with Pierce Brothers work.

Ah, well. She could do the whole thing by herself. It would just take more time. She didn't have to deliver for a client. This was her baby, and she intended to make sure her first house was filled with her trademark creativity and restoration materials. Besides saving buckets of money, it would give the place a personal touch every homeowner appreciated.

She made notes in her pad, sketching out various ideas for the rooms. The roof would need replacement, but the structure itself was solid. The shingles were basic brown and easy to fill in. The basement was small and stuffed with various junk and insects galore, but it wouldn't need to be gutted. Everything was salvageable. That was the primary reason she'd wanted the property.

Humming under her breath, she lost herself in the magic of endless possibilities, ending in the tiny bedroom off the Jack and Jill bathroom. Checking light fixtures and computing square feet, her brain clicked madly until she noticed something out of place.

A blanket with a small oil lamp was set up neatly in the corner. A pile of books lay by its side, stacked in perfect precision. Charlie frowned, walking over to examine the odd setup. The blanket didn't look old, and the books had no dust on them. The lamp seemed to have a surplus of fluid and looked recently used.

Odd. A chill ran down her spine. The house was set on a block far enough away from the occasional violence and drugs that sprung up on the outskirts of town, but what if her house was being used for squatters? Or people doing drugs?

Dragging in a breath, she inspected every inch of the house but found no proof of needles, weed, or any other paraphernalia that pointed to crime. The front door was locked, and the main windows were cracked but not busted open. Where was the point of entry? After another half hour, she came up empty. She shook her head, making a note to check on it more tomorrow, and headed back out.

Shadows were beginning to chase the sun down, but a few leftover rays warmed her face. She got in the truck and turned the key.

Nothing.

Ah, crap.

She tried again but got the grindy sound that confirmed she was going nowhere. Muttering a curse, she popped the hood. She went through her normal checklist of diagnostics but found nothing strange. Probably the battery. A simple jump would work, and she had the cables. She looked around, and with a sinking heart, realized no one was there to help. No doors to knock on, and she wasn't comfortable enough in the neighborhood to begin walking around. Better to just call in some help.

She grabbed her phone and tried Sydney first.

"Hello?"

"Syd, it's Charlie. Are you still at the office?"

"Yes, I'm working late tonight and Becca is with the sitter. What's up?"

"My car broke down and I think it needs a jump. I hate to bother you, but do you think you can come help me? I know Raven is at the bar, but I can check with Morgan if you can't get me."

"No, it's time I got out of here anyway. Give me the address." Charlie recited it to her. "I'll be there in fifteen."

"Thanks."

She clicked off, got back in the truck, and waited until she saw Sydney's car. She waved her friend over, directing her close to hook up the cables. "You rock. I didn't want to get stuck waiting for Triple *A*."

Sydney's green eyes filled with concern. "What are you doing out here?" she asked, her gaze taking in the empty street. "This place is deserted and on a dead end. You know there was a drug bust a few blocks over last week?"

Charlie laughed. "I'm fine. This is the new house I bought to flip." She waved her hand proudly in the air. "Gonna fix it up, make it nice, and sell it."

Her friend's mouth dropped open. "Girlfriend, please tell me you are not working on this all alone, late at night."

"Of course not. Eventually I'll hire some help, and it's not late at night. It's only seven pm."

Sydney crossed her arms in front of her chest and gave her *the look*. It reminded her a bit of her own mother. Since Sydney was a mother of a six-year-old, it wasn't a far reach. "This is dangerous," she said firmly. "I'm all about flipping houses and changing the neighborhood, but you didn't even tell anyone about it. Let us help."

"I'm fine, I swear. I like doing things on my own, and this is separate from Pierce Brothers work. Plus, I always carry pepper spray and a bat in case something happens. Can you gun your engine for me? I'm going to try to start it."

Grumbling under her breath, Sydney obeyed, and in a few minutes, the pickup roared back to life. Charlie shot her a thumbs-up signal and disconnected the cables. "Thanks so much. I'm good to go."

"I'm following you out of here. What made you buy this property?"

"It was the cheapest, and it has great potential. Look at the land." She pointed out the generous lot, infested with weeds, mud, and rocks. "Most of the houses in this area are squeezed tight together. Since this is on a dead end, it can be a great haven for someone who needs it."

Sydney shook her head. "You got it bad. A true rehab addict. Listen, I'm thrilled you're doing this on your own terms but you need to be safe. What if it's being used for other stuff like gangs or drugs?"

Her mind flashed to the quiet, neat corner with the books. "I didn't see any evidence of anything criminal. Just looks like a squatter needed a warm place to stay. I'm sure he or she will leave once I begin work."

Sydney's mouth dropped open. "Someone is living here!? What did you find?"

"Just a lamp and some books. I'm sure it's harmless."

Sydney frowned. "I'll help you with the project," she announced.

A pang of affection hit hard. She'd only been working with Sydney and the Pierce Brothers under a year, but already she felt as if she had a family. They took care of their own. "Syd, I adore you, but between work at Pierce and your daughter, you have no extra time. Besides, I want to do this on my own. Now stop being a worry wart and get your ass home."

Charlie blew her a kiss and got back into the truck. Finally, Sydney pulled out, carefully following her to the town limits before they went their separate ways. Charlie drove to her apartment with a smile on her face. It was nice to have friends who cared. She'd make sure she checked in with people when she was at the house and put an extra bottle of pepper spray inside. She'd learned in college how important it was to take care of herself. When an overly enthusiastic male backed her into a bedroom at a party, ignoring her repeated *no*'s, she'd lashed out and screamed *fire* at the top of her lungs until someone took notice.

He'd ended up with a social media smear as she warned everyone to stay far away from him.

Afterward, she'd taken defense classes so she felt more confident fighting back.

She pulled into her parking space and headed to her apartment. Immediately, the space settled and pulsed with warmth around her.

Kicking off her boots, she collapsed on the couch. Her place was cozy, with everything she needed to live happily, and dirt cheap. The apartment building might look like crap from the outside, but inside she had appliances, warmth, and wifi. She'd decorated the rooms with her usual creativity, and now it was a feast for the senses. She'd painted her own canvases and hung them on the walls, interspersed between photo collages and shelves containing fun trinkets. She'd sewn her own throw pillows in happy colors like lemon, lime, and tangerine, brightening up her dull beige sofa sleeper, which was the most comfortable thing she'd ever sat her ass on. Much better than Brady's Mercedes. The coffee and side tables were restored wood she'd refinished. The television was a much smaller screen than most people demanded, but it was clear and color and half price. The chandelier had been created by beads bought at the craft store, and matched the various genie lamps she'd grabbed at a garage sale. A few bucks of polish and some elbow grease had restored them to glory.

Her place was eclectic and fun and made her happy.

She wondered what Brady's place looked like.

The thought flickered so quickly, she jerked and pushed it out of her head. For the past week, they'd left each other alone. Everything was finally coming together for her. She'd carved out a place at Pierce Brothers, and she had her own house to flip.

She closed her eyes with a smile on her face and dreamed of a perfect future.

Chapter Four

"The dialogue between client and architect is about as intimate as any conversation you can have, because when you're talking about building a house, you're talking about dreams."—Robert A. M. Stern

Dalton peeked his head in. "Dude, Cal called an emergency conference. You free?"

Brady nodded, grateful for the interruption. He'd spent too many hours bent over his desk, gaze trained on his computer. "Anything wrong?"

"Don't know. Just said it was important."

"Okay, let me grab some coffee and I'll meet you in there." He headed to the kitchen, which was stocked with every piece of machinery needed to work 24/7. From the stainless steel refrigerator, cappuccino maker, soda machine, vending machines, and mahogany cupboards stuffed with goodies, everyone made sure cravings could be satisfied. He headed to his stock of specially ground Kenyan coffee, anticipating that first whiff of pure bliss, lifted the airtight cover, and found...something else.

He frowned and took a sniff. This wasn't his coffee. The scent of fake beans drifted to his nostrils, weak and wimpy and painful to his coffee-loving soul. Clenching his hands into tight fists, he marched to the front desk. "Rachel, why was my coffee switched out?" he demanded.

The older woman was in her sixties, but looked a decade younger. With smooth skin and a polished appearance, Rachel would be the one to know what he was talking about. She was ruthlessly organized and on top of supplies. A smile wreathed her face. "Charlie found a supplier who sold in bulk and saved us tons of money. She said it's exactly like the brand you like but half the price. Is it good?"

Son of a bitch. He glowered, trying to yank back his temper. "No."

Her face fell. "Oh. Well, I guess I can switch it back if you'd like." She paused. "Seems like a waste of money, though. Charlie said the amount we save could go toward the local pet shelter to help the animals. Wasn't that a great idea?"

His temper hitched a notch higher. Now she was spreading her frugality around the office. He gave plenty to charity, and he refused to have his few indulgences yanked from him. He'd already lost his pastries. "I'd appreciate if you switch it back."

She nodded, her eyes flaring with disapproval. "Of course."

"Thank you, Rachel." He headed toward the conference room, skipping the coffee. The men were already seated around the polished table. Cal took the head, sprawled out in his usual battered jeans, T-shirt, and work boots. Dalton was popping Hershey kisses into his mouth, looking the most relaxed of the crew. With his surfer hair caught in a man bun and long, tapered fingers drumming the table, he didn't seem nervous about the emergency meeting. Tristan sat between them, clad in his high-powered, custom suit. He sat completely still, a slight frown on his brow from the interruption of his tight, controlled schedule.

Brady took his customary place to Caleb's right. He'd grown up with these men and looked at them as family—not friends. He'd met Cal in college freshman year and been invited to his house for the weekend. Instantly, he'd clicked with all the brothers and began splitting his time between them and his family, who lived a few towns away. He'd been fascinated with Pierce Brothers Construction from the first day, loving the idea of working for a family firm. He got his degree, passed the architectural board tests, and was hired immediately by Cal's father, Christian.

Of course, the tight-knit family he'd signed on to had finally splintered into pieces after they'd lost their beloved mother, Diane Pierce, driving all the brothers in separate directions. Tristan had headed to New York City to do real estate, and Dalton fled to Florida to open a wood restoration business. Brady had stayed with Cal and become a constant in the business, drawing up all the plans for houses and even doing some home renovation when needed.

When Christian died of a heart attack, the will had stated the brothers must work together in the family business for one year or it would be sold. They'd agreed to do it, and after a hard road, they eventually forgave each other and moved onward. When Brady looked at all of them now, a sense of brotherly connection and fierce loyalty shimmered in the air. Having them all back was a gift. He was now a full partner in the company and helped drive all the decisions. He had everything he'd ever dreamed of—financial security, a job he loved, a dream house, and friends who were family.

If only he could find his damn wife.

He pushed his distracting thoughts out of his mind and concentrated on the conversation. As usual, Cal got straight to the point. "We have a problem with Charlie."

Dalton cocked his head in surprise. "What's the problem? I thought her work was stellar."

Brady jumped right in. "I knew it. I didn't want to be the one who said I told you so, but I had doubts from the beginning."

Cal rolled his eyes. "There's nothing wrong with her work. And I still don't understand why you two can't be in the same room together without sharing dirty looks. Sydney came to me about something that concerns me."

"Is she in trouble?" Tristan asked. Concern lit his amber eyes. "If she is, we'll help her."

"She bought a house on her own to flip."

Dalton grinned. "Good for her. She's come a long way since I met her."

Cal snorted. "And a longer time since you tried to make Raven jealous by pretending you were interested in Charlie. I still love that story."

"Didn't she give you a shove and a tongue blistering in the parking lot of My Place?" Tristan jumped in.

Dalton groaned. "Leave me alone. I was screwed up and didn't realize Raven was the love of my life. I paid for my sins."

Brady remembered Cal telling him about that incident. Seemed Dalton and Charlie became friends, but when he broke up with

Raven, he tried to use Charlie to make his ex-lover jealous. It backfired when Charlie confronted him, refusing to break female code and giving him a few hard truths.

Dalton's skin turned a shade red. "I should've never told you. I was drunk at the time."

"That's when we get all the good stuff," Tristan commented. "The Raging Bitch IPA does it every time."

Brady laughed. He was constantly entertained by the crew, but he brought back the purpose of the meeting. "So, Charlie bought a house to flip. Why is that a problem? Isn't she able to do her own sideline as long as it doesn't affect Pierce Brothers?"

"Yes, but I found out the property is on the outskirts of town in Trapps. I happened to do a drive-by today and several things concern me."

"That's not the best area," Tristan said. "It's pretty close to some of the hot spots. How many houses on the block?"

"Only a handful. It's on a dead-end street, so no immediate neighbors. Good lot. Crappy house, but structurally sound. Has potential," Cal said.

Tristan steepled his fingers. "She's got an eye for property."

Brady kept the surprise from showing on his face. He had no idea she had enough money to invest in her own house to flip, let alone know how to pick one. Sure, she was enthusiastic about her job, but he figured she wouldn't be around on a long-term basis. "Who's her crew?" Brady asked.

Cal leaned back in his chair. Worry glinted from gunmetal eyes. "No one. She's doing everything herself. Sydney says she intends to do her work in the early evenings after Pierce Brothers and on weekends."

Brady stared at Cal. "You mean she's working alone, in that neighborhood, at night?"

"That's right," Cal said.

Dalton groaned. "We can't let her do that. If something happens, we'll never forgive ourselves."

Cal nodded. "Agreed. Let's put a plan in place and bring her in for a discussion."

"Who do we have available to help her out?" Brady asked.

"Jason?" Tristan suggested.

"Nope, he's on a job for the next few weeks. Actually, all my main crew members are booked for the next two months."

"Maybe we can get her to delay the work," Brady said. "Wait until we can offer her some help."

Dalton shot him a look. "You don't know Charlie very well, do you, dude?"

He glowered. "I know she's a real pain in the ass."

Dalton grinned. "You like her."

His mouth fell open. He closed it with a snap, embarrassed at his obvious reaction. How juvenile. Dalton loved to jab at him and try to get him flustered. Some people thought it was part of his charm. "I have no opinion on her," he said way too stiffly. His dick stirred and screamed him a liar. Dammit, he had to focus on the problem at hand. "Dalton, why can't you give her a hand a few days per week?"

"Can't. I'm helping out Raven with the bar, building Cal and Morgan's new house, and have a ton of side jobs."

Cal rubbed his head. "It's the height of summer and we're at our peak. I'm slammed."

"Same here," Tristan said. "I'm traveling a lot and cramming in renovation on a few projects. There's just no damn time."

Silence settled. Very slowly, all the men swiveled their gaze to him. It took him a few moments to realize their intention.

"Hell, no," he bit out. "I work on renovation only when there's no other option."

"I think this fits the guidelines," Cal said. "You did mention you were caught up on most of our clients. Can you make the time?" Cal asked.

Frustration zipped through his blood. "I'm caught up, but there's always a ton of work. I can't afford to get behind by playing babysitter."

Dalton winced. "If she heard that, she'd come after all of us. She may be small, but Charlie is scary when she gets mad."

Brady smothered a groan at his friend's expression. When had they all become whipped by their women? Tristan seemed to be the only one left with some common sense, so he directed his words to him. "Look, I agree she needs someone at the site, but can't we hire an intern for her?"

Tristan regarded him thoughtfully. "Not a bad idea. I can ask around and see if there's an alternative. In the meantime, I think you'd be perfect to help her out. You can book your mornings out for clients, then spend late afternoon to evening working on the house. I'm sure I'll be able to find someone who wants extra money or to learn the trade."

"We'll help cover the overload on your work schedule," Cal added. "I just need to know you're on board before we bring Charlie in to tell her the plan."

The men around the table waited for his answer. A strange foreboding shivered down his spine, as if he knew things were about to change but he didn't know how. He quickly thought over his options and realized he had none. She couldn't be alone in that neighborhood, and he was the best one to help out until they found someone else. It would only be temporary. "I'll do it."

Cal let out a breath. "Thanks. I appreciate it. Now I just need to find the right way to tell her so it doesn't look like we're bullying or forcing her to accept help."

He shook his head. "Just explain to her it's not safe for a woman alone, plus she's getting free help. Win/win. She'll be grateful."

Cal and Dalton burst into laughter. He glared at them but noticed even Tristan was barely holding back a grin. "You really have no clue, do you?" Dalton asked. "I can't wait till you finally fall for some hot-tempered Latina woman who tells you how it really is."

He arched a brow. "I've always told you the perfect woman in my life not only respects my decisions, but listens. I have no problem claiming the leadership role."

Tristan lost the battle and grinned. "Can't wait to meet her. Guess you plan on being single a long damn time."

He shook his head at their good-natured jabbing. They'd been on his case for years about the type of woman he sought out, but Brady knew what was important to make a long lasting relationship. He'd seen it every day. If his father gave an order, everyone listened. Things ran smoothly and respect layered the relationship. Was that so bad? He wasn't some monster who wanted to order his lover around. He craved a give and take, with the knowledge he'd protect them both. It may be old-fashioned, but it wasn't wrong, and damned if he was going to keep apologizing for it.

"Okay, let's get this over with and call her in. I'll try to present it in the best way possible. Everyone ready?"

They nodded, and Cal opened the door to get her.

* * * *

Screw the Pierce Brothers.

Charlie seethed as her gloved hands began ripping out various junk from the house and dragging it to the dumpster. They had the nerve to summon her to the office and dictate who would help renovate her house? The house she'd invested in alone? And by renovate, they clearly meant babysit. A watcher. A keeper. Some big strong man to handle any trouble thrown her way, like she couldn't protect herself.

Hell, no.

Gritting her teeth, she threw her pissed-off energy into the cleanup, going over the entire episode in her head. Cal had taken the lead, but it was Brady's quiet judgment that made her crazy. He stared at her with a touch of disapproval, as if her rejection of their proposal was yet another stupid move she made because she wasn't smart enough to accept their help. He figured she'd be grateful. When she'd thrown it right back and told them no, thank you, they had the gall to practically threaten her. It had gone so bad she'd stormed out, almost tempted to quit and go on her own.

Almost.

But she needed this job. She wasn't far enough along on her own, and Pierce Brothers had the perfect setup. It would be easier to quit if she thought she was being placated by men who didn't respect her, but deep inside, she knew that wasn't the case. They were protective of all their employees, and had clearly explained they only wanted to be sure she was safe in the neighborhood. Yes, she appreciated their concern, but she wanted to do this job herself.

At least she'd made her opinion quite clear when she politely thanked them for their concern and promised to kick anyone's ass who showed up on her job site without prior approval.

Yeah. That had gone real well.

Blowing out a breath, she spent the next hour moving crap into the dumpster, only pausing for a water break. The junk removal was the easy part. She needed to attack the wall dividing the kitchen and family room, but she'd need a set of finalized plans. She refused to ask Brady for a favor, and if she paid him, he'd only treat her like a chore rather than a client. Her backup architect wasn't as good but would have to do. Then she'd concentrate on getting rid of the crap cabinets. She had her eye on some functional, low-cost ones at Anthony's in stark white. It would brighten the place up. She guzzled water, enjoying the silence. Dalton always worked with boy bands blaring, and Cal loved his metal eighties stuff, but she loved the quiet. Nothing needed but the flow of her thoughts and the movements of her hands as she restored and rebuilt. Her soul practically sang amidst the sawdust, mold, and rotted wood.

She was on her last trip when she spotted the small shadow on the front lawn, staring at her. A young boy—definitely a teen—stood on her property, a shocked look on his face. Seemed he hadn't expected her presence. He had large, dark eyes, beautiful brown skin, and long, lanky legs. He wore black cargo shorts, a gray T-shirt, and orange and white sneakers. Resentment practically beamed her like a laser. Obviously, she wasn't wanted. "Hi," she called out. "I'm Charlie."

He blinked but didn't move. Shifted his weight back and forth on those fancy sneakers. "What are you doing here?" His voice held the sharp edge of youth, with the high pitch of puberty. "This ain't your property."

She regarded him curiously, sensing no aggression but more of a possessive inflection of tone. "Actually, it is," she said lightly. Tugging off her gloves, she took a few steps closer. "I bought it. Plan on renovating it and selling. Are you from this neighborhood?"

He jerked back, averting his gaze, but not before she caught the flare of anger and grief in his dark eyes. Ah, she'd finally figured out who her visitor had been. The books, the lamp, and the blanket told her he'd been using her house as a crash pad. Normally, she'd let it go and urge him to be on his way, but something about the boy called to her.

Hands clenched into fists, body tight, he seemed to fight with himself before shaking his head and pivoting on his sneaker-clad heel. "Nah. Forget it." He'd taken a few steps before she called out again.

"It's your books in my house, isn't it? *The Outsiders*?"

He stiffened, slowly turning back around. He lifted his head with pure rebellion. "Yeah. It is. I wasn't trespassing. Didn't know anyone lived there."

"I know. I just recently bought it. Was trying to figure out how someone got in there."

He shrugged. "It was open."

Her lips twitched. "Oh, my bad. Do you like the book?"

He blinked. "Huh?"

"*The Outsiders*. It was on the top of your stack. Surprised you're reading it."

"'Cause you don't think kids like me can read? Think I'm more into comic books?"

She jerked back, frowning. His tone shimmered with resentment. "No. I didn't think the book was well known in your generation. Figured it was a bit out of date, you know? It's from the eighties. And I take offense to both statements. A kid is a kid, and comic books rock."

Her words had the intended reaction. A quick grin slid across his lips before quickly being squashed. She wondered why he was holing up in an abandoned house. Trouble at home? Friends? School? It could be anything, but he'd be prickly if she didn't mind her business.

"I saw it on TV," he admitted. "Looked cool. The book's good."

"I had such a crush on Matt Dillon when I first saw it," she sighed.

He rolled his eyes. "Can I have my stuff back or you gonna call the cops?"

"Nothing to call the cops for if the house wasn't locked. Come on in." She turned and went inside, not stopping to see if he followed. Slowly, he trudged through the sagging door, his gaze taking in the space now cleared of junk.

"Where's the other people?" he asked.

"It's just me. You gotta problem with that?"

Again, that grin came and went. Charlie liked the way it softened his features and took away the edges. "No, just seems like a lot of work to rebuild a house where it's only gonna get trashed again."

"Why? The neighborhood is solid enough. I figured a family will want in, and I like the property. I also intend to renovate it, which is quite different from a rebuild. Besides, you must like something about it to be hanging around."

He studied her with a gaze way too shrewd for his age. "I like a place where no one bothers me. You really think someone will buy it?"

"I really do." She crossed her arms in front of her chest. "I'll even make you a deal."

Right away, he stepped back, poised to run out of the house. "Don't make no deals."

She nodded. "Good. Means you're smart. Just saying if you're ever interested in seeing how to renovate, I'll show you some stuff."

"You don't even know me."

She shrugged. "Just an idea. If you have nothing to do, I'll be here working every day from 4 pm on. Got electricity now so no need for the oil lamp. But you can't sneak in anymore. And I don't allow friends or anyone else on my property when I'm not around. If I find that, I will call the cops. I have to be careful, too."

Interest flashed over his face. "What kind of stuff?"

"I'm tearing down that wall, then gutting the kitchen."

"With big machines?" he asked.

She laughed. "Nah, with my sledgehammer."

His eyes widened. Interesting. Too many kids weren't keen on manual labor. They liked sleek computers, video games, YouTube, instant gratification, and conversations that never occurred face to face. Renovating a house bored them to tears. Hell, she didn't judge. She had been the oddball her whole life. But if this kid wanted to learn, she'd love the company.

Much better than Brady Heart.

"I'll think about it," he stated.

"Cool. Let me get your stuff." She returned with the blanket, lamp, and books and stuck them in a plastic grocery bag. "What time does school let out?"

"Three. I have basketball on Tuesdays and Thursdays."

"If you want to work here, you need to let your mom and dad know."

"Mom doesn't come home till six."

"How old are you?"

The defenses shot back up. "Old enough."

Latchkey kid. Most were with both parents needing to work.

She'd been the same, sometimes staying alone till late, making her own dinner and putting herself to bed. She was used to her own company and had no issues or excuses about being abandoned. Her mother had done her best and given her all. Charlie had been one of the lucky ones. She backed off, not wanting to spook him. "I know. I was ten when I started staying by myself."

He studied her face, finally nodding. His shoulders relaxed. "I'm thirteen."

"Ugh. Crappy age."

He laughed, seeming surprised. "Better go. Thanks."

"Hey, what's your name?"

"Jackson."

"Good to meet you, Jackson. Hope I'll see you here so I can get a little help."

He lifted a hand in the air and disappeared through the door. She thought about him for a while, wondering about his circumstances, wondering why he intrigued her. Maybe she'd see him again. Maybe not. Either way, at least she wasn't spooked about her mysterious visitor any longer.

If she told Brady, would he back off?

Probably not. He pictured himself the white knight ready to rescue a damsel, except it wasn't in a castle with a dragon, but a dilapidated house on a back end alley.

She checked again on her stash of pepper sprays readily available and her baseball bat leaning against the entrance to the kitchen. Hmm, if she wrapped it in barbed wire, would it be extra scary? Like Lucille from *The Walking Dead*?

Nah, that'd just be more like serial killer.

A giggle burst from her lips as she imagined Brady catching sight of her with a deadly bat. His appalled face would be almost worth it.

She glanced at her watch and figured she'd squeeze out another hour. Might as well hit the gross, scary, serial killer basement.

Glancing back and forth in the quiet, she grabbed her pepper spray just in case and headed down the rickety stairs.

Chapter Five

"Each new situation requires a new architecture."—Jean Nouvel

Brady stared at the house and wondered what the woman had gotten herself into.

Trapps wasn't the best area to begin with. Drug dealers were known to haunt the adjoining neighborhood, and it was all too possible for them to wander over to expand their distribution. His assessing gaze took in the structure, and he began a slow inspection around the property, noting the half-full dumpster. Hmm, she'd gotten a lot done. Of course, after she'd stormed out of the conference room, why wasn't he surprised she'd decided to work alone as a big "screw you" to everyone?

The house was small but solid. At least she got that right. The outside would need to be stripped and re-sided or painted. The lot was extra large for this area, but was now filled with overgrown weeds and creatures who probably had made a happy home. The cracked windows needed replacing, and so did the roof. He hoped she hadn't invested in a house with electrical or plumbing issues. That'd be the main costs. Surface was easy enough. Bad wires, pipes, or mold killed you each and every time.

Guess he'd find out now.

He shook his head. Honestly, she was acting like a child. He didn't want to be here either, but it was best to have some type of buddy system in a questionable neighborhood, especially when working alone at night. Did she want to court trouble for attention?

Or was she so selfish she didn't care about anyone else who'd worry about her?

Tamping down a sigh, he knocked on the front door, already prepped for her attitude. She'd be pissed he showed up, but he'd made a promise to his friends, and he was sticking with it.

She didn't answer.

He knocked again, but after a few moments, he turned the doorknob and let himself in. The creak in the air should have alerted her, but when he called out her name, there was only silence. Where was she? And didn't she have the sense to lock the damn door? Sydney had told him about the mysterious visitor Charlie didn't seem to be worried about. What if the person consistently breaking in decided to pay her an impromptu visit? Smothering a curse, he walked further, examining the rooms.

Definite possibilities were here. It could be a cozy family home, even though the bedrooms were small and the kitchen needed updating. He took his time investigating, until he finally heard a clatter rise from the basement. Hmm, she probably hadn't heard him come in. Real smart. Thank God he'd shown up because she definitely couldn't be trusted to work here alone. His temper simmered at just the thought of the trouble she could be in if he'd been someone dangerous.

And then he saw the baseball bat.

His mouth fell open. Propped up in the corner, the large wooden bat was the perfect extra addition to help a criminal get further. He pressed his lips together, fighting the urge to throw open the basement door and stomp downstairs, giving her the scare of a lifetime.

Would serve her right.

He picked up the bat, running his hands down the smooth surface, and moved back into the kitchen. Who'd done her architectural plans? And why the hell wouldn't she have asked him? Irritation prickled his nerves. She might not like him, but he figured he'd earned her respect with his work. Did she dislike him so much she refused to ask him for sketches? They were coworkers, and he wouldn't have charged her.

Finally, he heard the door open to the basement. He opened his mouth to call out her name, then decided not to warn her. Maybe if he startled her, she'd realize anyone could have just walked right in the front door and availed himself of her only weapon.

He took a few steps into the family room, his shoes creaking slightly over the worn floors.

"Aghgh!"

Before he even managed to clear the corner, the warrior shriek hit his ears at the same time a foot smashed into his crotch. Exploding pain crippled his balls. The bat clattered to the ground. He bent over, grabbing his poor dick, which had retreated into his intestines.

Blinking through the agony, he tried to speak but a sudden shock of spray blasted his vision.

He didn't remember if he screamed or not. Later on, he'd deny it on the Bible, not even caring if his mother promised a trip to hell for lying to God. At that very moment, hell was right in front of him, with his streaming eyes and throbbing dick, and snot pouring from his nose. He stumbled back, his ears ringing, and began rubbing furiously at his eyes, completely blinded.

"Brady!"

The feminine voice barely registered. He was intent on trying to live past the agony. His brain splintered on which was worse—his burning eyes or his weeping testicles.

"Oh, my God. I'm so sorry! Oh, my God, I thought you were a criminal! Here, sit down. I'll call 911. Do you need an ambulance? A doctor? Oh, my God!"

The words bubbled in the air and he desperately tried to make sense of them. Strong hands grasped him and lowered him to the filthy floor. A bunch of towels were pressed into his grip, and he tried to dab at his stinging eyes. His tear ducts had exploded, and wetness dripped down his cheeks. Had that whimper come from him?

So embarrassing.

"What the fuck did you do to me?" he managed to grate out.

"Pepper spray." She shoved something at him, but he couldn't see it. "Here, hold your head back. I'm going to pour water in your eyes to see if I can flush it out."

"Son of a bitch!"

The water hit his eyeballs and more stinging commenced. He

uttered a stream of Spanish—the only damn words he remembered were the curses—and wondered if Charlotte Grayson had not only taken away his vision but also his ability to ever pleasure a woman again. He craved to crawl into a ball and be left alone, but she kept pouring water on him, wiping at his snotty nose and edging way too close to his injured anatomy.

"The spray is only supposed to be temporary, but let me take you to the hospital. You look terrible."

He still couldn't see her face, just a rough shadowed outline of her figure. "You kicked me in the balls and sprayed me with that shit!" he bellowed. "Are you crazy? And I'm not going to the hospital." If anyone got wind of this story, he'd be done. He'd never live down the gossip.

"You broke in! I came up from the basement and heard a noise and saw a shadow holding my bat. I thought you were going to kill me!"

"You left the fucking front door open! I knocked, but when you didn't answer, I came right in. You would've been dead if I had been a killer."

Was that a snort or was he imagining things? "Doesn't seem like it. Looks more like you would've been going straight to jail since I took you out."

Rage mixed with pain. He reached his hands out toward the fuzzy figure in an effort to throttle her, but she jerked out of his reach. "You took me by surprise," he managed to choke out. "If I'd been a real killer, I wouldn't have waited. I would've trapped you in the basement."

"That's why I brought the pepper spray down with me. And I did lock the front door. Hmm, I wonder if that's how Jackson was getting in. Probably need to install a new dead bolt. I'll get that done by morning."

Was she trying to have a rational conversation with him or had his head truly exploded? He had no idea how long it took him to stumble to his feet, but he shook off her efforts to help and leaned weakly against the wall, fluid still streaming from his membranes. "Pepper spray won't stop a killer," he muttered, swiping at his eyes and nose. "You stormed out of the conference room like a toddler."

Through a haze of fuzz, her mouth dropped open. He couldn't

mistake the fury laced in her tightly wound tone. "Maybe if you didn't treat me like a toddler, I wouldn't have to act like one. No one has any right to tell me what I can do with my own property. Or act like a bunch of overprotective big brothers bossing me around. Hell, no. I've got it handled. Now, are you going to the hospital or not?"

He glared through his tears. "Not. I'm fine. Just need to let the stuff work its way out. Funny, I seem to remember them taking you in for an internship and never treating you like an outsider. Cal and Dalton and Tristan trust you. You're not just a worker there anymore, Charlie. You're family. Don't you get it yet?"

A brief silence settled. Oh, good. He'd managed to counter some of that stubborn rebellion. A flash of admiration shot through him, taking him off guard. What was that about? Yes, he liked her spunk, even if it was a tad too intense. Yes, he respected her work ethic and pride and vision. It was a quality he didn't see very often, in either men or women. Maybe that's why it was hard for him to deal with. Not that he had to. If she was his woman, he wouldn't allow her to be fixing up some old house in a crappy neighborhood without supervision. End of argument.

But she wasn't his woman and that was good.

This time when she spoke, her words were a bit softer. "I appreciate it. I do, but you have to understand I'm used to running my own life. How would you feel if you had a project that was important to you and Cal decided you needed a supervisor?"

He'd be pissed. Her point hit home. Brady wiped his eyes, finally able to see her form more clearly. "I get it. Listen, I'm asking you to let me help. Not because I think you can't do this on your own, but if something were to happen, none of us would forgive ourselves. You're one of us now. That means we help each other out. Who's doing your plans?"

She rocked back and forth and took a while before answering. "Don't know yet."

"You don't trust me with your house?"

"No, you're a great architect. I just don't want you to feel obligated, especially if I change stuff."

A flash of regret hit him. He'd been a bit hard on her. "I won't. I'll do the plans at no charge, and I'll help you renovate in the evenings. I'm sure you could use an extra hand."

"I've never seen you involved in renovation. You never leave the office."

She sounded slightly accusatory, which made his lips twitch. "I've done rehab in the past when needed. I prefer the office, but sometimes it's good to switch things up. Get my hands dirty."

Was she nibbling at her lip? His vision was still blurred and the burning pain lingered. How long would it take for this crap to leave his system? "We can try things out," she finally said. "After a week, we'll reassess."

She didn't trust him at all. Not that he blamed her. Maybe it was the sexual attraction that threw him off. Being mean because he wanted to drag her into bed. God, how juvenile. Like pulling a girl's hair because he liked her. He'd thought he was better than that.

Evidently not.

"Agreed. Let's get the new deadbolt installed before anything else. I'll draw up plans once you tell me what your vision is. Who's Jackson?"

"Oh, I figured out who was breaking into the house. Young teen. He'd been using the house for some alone time. Brought his books and stuff. I offered to let him help me work on the house if he wanted."

He frowned. "Think that's a good idea when you don't even know him? He could be into drugs or staking out the house to bring his friends over. You can't trust everyone you meet."

She laughed, surprising him. "I don't. I go with a gut feeling, and this one told me he may like learning how to renovate. He may not even come back."

Another good reason he'd be here to help. "We'll see."

They fell quiet. He sensed her studying him for a while, but he was oddly comfortable under her stare. "I'll need something from you though, in order to move forward."

Suspicion leaked through him. "What?"

Her grin was pure cheekiness. "Admit I kicked your ass."

He couldn't help but laugh. Damn, she really had given it to him. "Only if you promise not to tell anyone. My man card may get yanked."

"We'll see how much you piss me off."

He shook his head, wiping his face with the towel one more

time. Finally, his balls had stopped throbbing and tentatively lowered back down. She had a wicked kick. "Fine. You grabbed your opportunity and took me down temporarily."

She pursed her full, candy-pink lips and blew out a breath in disgust. "That was a sucky admission."

"Best you're gonna get after you almost castrated me."

"Whiner."

He laughed again. "Can we get out of here, please? Call it a night?"

"Sure. Let me just dump this last batch from the basement. Do you need me to drive you home or can you see?"

"I'm fine." He moved a bit slowly, but by the time she was done, he felt able to see enough of the road. "We can work up the plans tomorrow."

"Okay." She paused by her ugly red truck. "I'm really sorry. I never meant to hurt you like that."

He waved a hand in the air. "Raven would be proud of you. Let's just hope my date tonight doesn't notice I look hungover."

"Date?"

Her surprise made him frown. "Yeah. There're actually women out there who like my company and don't want to pepper spray me."

She laughed. "Got it. Have fun."

She got in her truck and drove off.

At least they'd come to some agreement. The Pierce brothers would be happy it was settled and they got to help her out. And Brady could handle a few evenings per week in her company. In fact, this strange attraction might fade after spending some time with her. This might be the best thing for him.

He drove home to get ready for his date, trying not to be concerned at his total lack of enthusiasm. This was his third date with Marissa, and she had all the qualities he was looking for. Besides being a stunning, quiet beauty, she was intelligent, soft spoken, and completely on board with a traditional type of relationship. He'd been thinking of seducing her tonight now that they'd gotten to know each other, but he always let his gut lead depending on what he sensed his woman wanted, or more important, needed.

He just hoped his poor dick was up for it after Charlie.

Chapter Six

"One of the great beauties of architecture is that each time it is like life starting all over again."—Renzo Piano

"Ready for the reveal?"

She took a deep breath and nodded. "Bring it on."

She tugged on her work gloves and tried to wipe off the sweat pouring from her forehead. August was a bitch in the northeast. Muggy, clingy heat kept the air heavy. She'd heard the West brag about their dry heat, but nothing was worse than a hot day in Connecticut when the air thickened and refused to move. Especially when working in a house with no A/C.

They'd done the complete walk-through, finalized plans, and finished up cleaning out the basement from hell. Now, it was time to rip out the carpets and see how bad the floors were. Sure, she always hoped for actual wood to refinish, but if they were bad, she'd just invest in new carpeting. Still, her heart beat with the thrill of the unknown and what could be.

They cut away the edges and pulled together, taking their time until the muddy, crusted fibers were carted away and the floors were naked to the vision.

She studied the faded wood, a dull oak color, walking around to examine the edges. Looking up, she broke into a joyous smile. "They're gorgeous! A little re-sanding and stain and we have new floors!"

Brady nodded, a small smile on his lips. "You got lucky."

"Hell, yes, I got lucky!" She broke into a happy dance, swinging her hips and waving her hands in the air to the music she heard in her head. "This is going to be awesome. Good floors automatically raise the investment value. Mo' money, mo' money! Come on—do the money dance with me."

He shook his head but she didn't care. She bet the man didn't even know how to dance. Poor thing. Charlie knew she could never get serious with a man who couldn't accomplish some badass moves on the dance floor. It spoke of a confidence and eroticism that was important in a relationship, at least to her. Plus, she refused to go through life dancing alone at weddings, parties, and all social functions.

His assessing gaze swept over her figure. Lush, dark lashes lowered to mask his expression. "I wouldn't get overexcited. The bathrooms aren't terrible and the pipes are decent, thank God. But the kitchen will cause you trouble. Did you see the cabinets? They're unsalvageable, and that wall boxing in the kitchen is load bearing. It can't come down, and it's a complete eyesore."

She stopped dancing and crossed her arms in front of her chest. "Boy, are you a Debbie Downer. I know, but I'm thinking of a plan."

"The roof needs replacement and so do the windows. Plus the shingles are crap."

"Waaa, waaa, waaa."

Was that amusement glinting in those sooty eyes or just her imagination? He turned and bent to pull the last rug remnants away, causing those jeans to stretch over his ass, emphasizing the muscled curves. Damn, he had a smokin' hot body. She liked seeing him in casual clothes for a change—even though his jeans weren't faded or old and his navy blue T-shirt seemed freshly pressed, even in the crippling heat. But he still cut an impressive figure, whether dressed in those sharp business suits or down-to-earth outdoor work clothes. It was an elemental male dominance in his aura he carried with him, as if he assumed everyone around would do his bidding. Probably another quality that made him so successful.

He walked back in and pointed to the entrance to the kitchen. "You want to knock this one down, right?"

"Definitely."

"You'll lose cabinet space."

"I can live with that. I have some ideas. Can you help me with the last of the basement junk? Then we can attack the wall tomorrow."

"Sure."

She grabbed her bat and pepper spray, ignoring his eye roll, and headed down the rickety stairs to the serial killer basement. At least it was unfinished space, which could house the washer and dryer, and eventually be converted into a family room. The last of the shelving held an array of mismatched paint cans, poles, boxes, and various junk. Grabbing a few boxes, they began sorting.

The question popped out before she had a chance to think about it. "I never asked you about your date last week. How was it?"

He arched a brow, not pausing in his pace. "Good."

"Steady girlfriend or new prospect?"

"Third date."

"Ah, the closer."

"Huh?"

She grinned, pushing the stray tendrils of hair from her eyes. "You know, the third date rule? You either sleep with them or decide to move on. What'd you decide?"

He stopped, gazing at her with faint astonishment. "Do you really ask anything that pops into your head or do you just like shocking people?"

"Don't think it's that shocking. Why are you so uptight?"

"I'm not uptight. I just happen to respect a person's privacy, which evidently, you do not. Some topics are inappropriate."

She snorted. Oh, he was fun to torture. "Nothing wrong with being honest and asking what you're genuinely curious about. I'm trying to get to know you better. I pretty much know nothing about you other than you're an architect. Oh, and you curse in Spanish when you're pissed, and look Latino but of course you're not."

He cut her an irritated glance. "I am Latino. And sometimes people don't want to share personal things with strangers. It's a matter of trust."

"How can you build trust if you don't take a risk and try to share things that are important to you?"

"It's called time. Obviously, you're young and impatient."

"Does that mean you're old and slow?" She smothered a

delighted grin as he actually humphed. Maybe working with him wasn't so bad. It was certainly amusing. "Sorry, I couldn't resist. How can you be Latino with a name like Brady Heart?"

"Brady is a nickname. My grandfather was English and my grandmother Latina. They had three sons, one being my father. My father married a Latina, but I still inherited my grandfather's English name."

She cocked her head, fascinated. "What's your birth given name?"

He stiffened. "I don't share that with anyone."

"Oh, my God. Is it something really bad? Like Dudley? Or Dick?"

"No, and I'm not discussing it further."

"Gaylord? Elmo?"

"No."

She wrinkled her nose. "Well, now you got me all curious, and I won't rest until I figure it out."

Suddenly, all that seething dark intensity turned on her. His eyes gleamed with warning, and his figure radiated with shocking energy. Her breath caught in her lungs at the sudden change. His voice lowered to a rich, gravelly velvet that shot shivers down her spine. "I'd be very careful, Charlotte," he warned. "There are certain things that shouldn't be challenged."

Electricity crackled between them. His gaze held hers and dug deep, and yearning rose inside her for something she didn't understand. She shifted her feet. "I told you I don't like that name."

A smirk touched those carved lips. "I do. It's elegant. Musical. Traditional."

She snorted. "Everything I'm not and that's why I hate it." Odd, though. For some reason, her belly dropped when he spoke her name. It seemed almost…intimate. She shook off the strange energy between them and went back to her interrogation. "Do you speak Spanish?"

"Only a few phrases. My parents only spoke English in our household. Though my father calls my mother *querida*."

She smiled. "I like that. I always wanted to learn another language but I barely made it through English class. Do you have brothers or sisters?"

"Two sisters."

"Younger? Older? Are you close?"

He gave a long-suffering sigh, as if the whole getting-to-know-you game was beginning to wear on his nerves. "Older. They're both married with kids."

"I bet your mama wanted that third date to work out for you, then."

He laughed, and her heart leapt at the sound. She liked making him laugh. He was so serious all the time. She wondered who was able to lighten him up besides the Pierce brothers. Of course, she'd caught him teasing Sydney and Morgan on occasion, but he'd always been so closed off around her. It was interesting to think there were other layers hidden under that starched shirt.

"I love my mama, but I know exactly what I'm looking for."

They finished two boxes and started on the next round. Oh, this was too interesting not to investigate. "Well, now you need to tell me what you're looking for in a woman."

"Why?"

"I'm curious. Women are always curious about what men are interested in." She threw up her hands at his suspicious look. "I swear I won't judge."

"Why don't you tell me what you're looking for first?" he challenged.

She dropped a rusty lawn sign into the box. "Fair enough. Unlike you, I have nothing to hide and don't mind people asking questions. I think it's a fascinating study in human behavior and figuring out our deepest needs."

"You're stalling."

She screwed up her face and went over her mental list. "Well, I want a man who has a great sense of humor and doesn't take himself too seriously."

"Serious how? Like ego? Pride in his work? In his manhood?"

She blinked. "Umm, you know, someone who can make me laugh and doesn't think he's better than me."

"Ah, so you don't like a man with an inflated ego."

"Right."

"Go on."

Off balance, she went back to her list. "A man who's open to explore various paths in his life with his career."

"A Peter Pan, huh?"

She stopped, cutting him a glare. "What are you talking about? That's not a Peter Pan."

"Sure it is. You're just sugarcoating it. You're saying you don't want a man to commit to a serious career path and pursue it even though there are obstacles. Sounds like you enjoy those starving, brooding artist types." He gave a shudder of distaste. "Good luck."

She gasped. "You're twisting my words! I'm talking about being open minded to life's curve balls and able to adapt to change."

"That's different than what you originally said. Do you mean a man who can fall on bad times but is able to focus on the good for both him and his partner?"

Did she? Yeah, that sounded better, somehow, but she didn't like the way he was hijacking her list and bending it to his will. "Yes, that's what I said."

"I must've misunderstood. Continue."

"This one is very specific but important. I want a man who can dance."

His groan snapped her temper. "Wait, let me guess. You want some *Dirty Dancing* dude to sweep you off your feet, believing if he's good on the dance floor, he's good in bed."

Her cheeks turned red. Ugh. How did he make it sound so...lame? He was probably mad because he couldn't dance, so he was trying to make her feel guilty. The words practically sputtered out of her mouth. "No! I just believe a man who can dance is confident and assured and not afraid what everyone else thinks of him."

"What if he just happens not to have rhythm and doesn't want to embarrass YOU? If you meet this perfect man and he sucks on the dance floor, you'd cut him loose?"

She squirmed. "No. Yes. I mean, it depends. It may not be a make or break, but it's a quality I look for. Is that okay with you? Can I get back to my final requirement, please?"

"Of course. I apologize. I'm dying to know what comes next."

She yanked out a carton of old rusty tools and dropped them with a loud clatter. "Gee, thanks. A man who makes me happy." She tossed him a triumphant look. He couldn't pull that one apart.

Brady frowned. "That's not a serious requirement. In fact, it's quite juvenile."

She spun around and shot him a nasty glare. "Excuse me?"

He ignored her, continuing to throw things at the box without even glancing over. "Someone who makes you happy is a total cop-out. What if you're wrong or disagree with his thoughts or actions? He's not making you technically happy at the moment, but he's doing it for the greater good because he loves you. You can't be happy all the time. Relationships grow and change and arc. That's what makes them interesting. Being happy all the time is a lukewarm quality on your list. Frankly, I'm disappointed. I expected so much more from you. I think we're done here. I'll start bringing the stuff to the dumpster."

And with that, he pivoted on his heel, grabbed the box, and headed upstairs.

She stared at the empty basement, frustration and temper whirling in choppy waves through her body, and wished to God she could hit him with the pepper spray again.

Oh, she so didn't like him.

* * * *

Brady tried not to laugh at her obvious ploy to ignore him and take the higher road. She was so delightfully emotional, it was impossible for her to hide her disdain and temper at his dismissing words. He knew she was dying for him to share his own list of traits but he didn't offer and she was stuck with the silent treatment for a while, so she had to just suck it up.

Damn, she was sexy.

Her shirt was canary yellow with hot pink piping. The deep *V* at the neck hinted at a yellow bra that was driving him a tad insane. What woman wore a yellow bra? Did her panties match? He'd always been a man who preferred black for its sexy sophistication. What was happening to him? Her jeans had holes in the knees and flared at the ankle. When she bent over, he noticed the pockets had bright rhinestone bling in the shape of hearts. Her work boots were pink, which reminded him of Morgan. He wondered if she ordered them from the same place.

Her multi-hued blonde hair was pulled back in a high ponytail, and her face was free of makeup. Those huge hazel eyes dominated her face and were so expressive it was like looking into the windows of her soul, just like the cliché. It was rare he saw a woman without polish or cosmetics as a barrier. Was she so confident in her looks, or did she truly not care what others thought? If it was the latter, was it possible she had that much freedom in her soul?

Freedom in the soul translated to freedom in the bedroom. Freedom to all possibilities on the physical and emotional plane. Freedom to every erotic demand he wanted to give her.

His dick sprang to life, and he smothered a groan. Holy hell, he needed to get himself under control. Playing a good game of banter was one thing. Getting intrigued by her sweet body was another. They'd never cross that line for a variety of reasons, but the biggest one hit him as hard in the balls as her kick had.

She wasn't interested.

She looked upon him as a tightass. Too old. Too rigid. Too judgmental. She dreamed of a creative soul who'd torture her and present pain as passion, twisting her up inside and then saying his good-bye. He'd seen it before, many times. But it wasn't his damn business, and he wasn't getting involved in anything other than renovating this house.

Focus was the key. Having some fun along the way would make it interesting, but he knew he had to watch himself. She was too tempting, and she was too damn much trouble.

He wanted a wife, not a roll in the hay, no matter how mind blowing it might be.

He repeated the mantra to himself and got back to work.

Chapter Seven

"Renovating old homes is not about making them look new... it is about making new unnecessary."—Ty McBride

"I'm going to restore the cabinets."

His look was all too familiar, and one she was well versed in. "Those can't be saved," he clipped out. His hand ran over the chipped façade of cheap green paneling and the torn linoleum countertops. The knobs were busted, and the insides were torn up. "You told me you were getting rid of them. In fact, this whole kitchen is a problem. There's not enough space for a table. Little storage, especially if we remove that wall."

"I've been thinking about it all night." Her irritation with him had finally faded enough and taken on another outlet. Since he refused to leave her side as her protector, she'd work him to death and satisfy her curiosity. It had a double bang effect since it would annoy the crap out of him. She'd been way too much of an easy target and he'd played her well a few days ago. Now, she'd gotten her composure back and realized his game.

She was going to play better.

Charlie bounced on her heels, channeling her favorite Pooh character, Tigger, and expounded on her brilliant idea. "You know all that wood I made you save from the basement?"

"The scraps I advised you to get rid of that are now cluttering up the yard?"

"Yes, those. I'm going to do a two-pronged approach. First, I'm keeping the top tier of cabinets because they're the best of the worst. I'll strip off the surface, put in new shelves and knobs, and paint them bright white."

"Why don't you get new ones?"

"Too expensive."

"It still won't be enough. You need to add bottom cabinets or the buyers will have nothing. It'll devalue the house."

"Ah, but I have a plan! I'm going to use the scrap wood from the basement and build them a corner cabinet here"— she pointed to the dead space on the end of the main counter—"and I'll make all the counters a beautiful stained plank wood."

He examined the space, his face doubtful. "You're going to give it a farmhouse look? Doesn't fit with the rest of the house."

"Not done. I'm going to build a high-top counter from that old headboard I snatched from that amazing store—the Barn—and put in stools. It gives eating space, modernizes the kitchen, and keeps it from being too farm looking."

He didn't answer, taking in her suggestions with a seriousness she was getting used to. She understood now Brady needed time to process all her ideas. Her brain worked different, exploding into a riot of color and graphics she made sense of. He needed time and space before the vision took hold. These past few days had given her a better glimpse into his work habits. "Maybe."

"Not done," she sang, clapping her hands together and dancing to the back of the kitchen. "See this here? I'm going to take the two windows I'm tearing out and make them a built-in cupboard for the rest of their storage."

He blinked. "You're taking those awful windows and turning them into a cupboard?"

"Yes! I've done it before and it's a great way to save money. We just have to make sure when we remove the windows we don't chip or break around the frame."

"I've never seen that done before. Won't it look cheap?"

"No. I've been studying renovation with old materials for a while now. I can make it look seamless."

"What about that dead wall?" He pointed to the massive empty space doing nothing but choking off the room. "There's no painting or built-in that will make that wall look good. Especially when people are eating at the counter with nothing to look at."

"I found the solution. I'm going to paint a graffiti design mural on it."

She hugged herself with excitement, waiting him out. The seconds dragged into minutes. Finally, he gazed at her with an expression of pure horror.

"You're kidding."

"No! I'm going to paint a big-assed, gorgeous graffiti-type wall in the kitchen. Isn't that genius? Brilliant?"

"You can paint? Graffiti?"

"Of course I can paint. You should see my apartment. I made these fabulous paintings out of old pizza boxes."

"No, I mean you're an artist-type painter? You studied art?"

She rolled her eyes. "No, I didn't actually study it, but I make things all the time and I know I can pull this off. What do you think?"

"I think you've officially lost your mind. If you're stuck on this idea, hire a real artist." He walked out of the kitchen, shaking his head. She followed him, refusing to be deterred.

"Too expensive. You need to think outside the box, Brady. I'm telling you, I can pull it off."

"I believe you think you can, but I've never seen a house with a graffiti wall in the kitchen. Or old windows converted into cupboards."

"It's gonna be awesome. For now, I don't want you worrying your pretty little head about it. We have a wall to take down and cabinets to work on."

He glared. "I'm not worried. This is your world. I'm just living in it."

"Cute. Let's remove the last of the counter from the kitchen so we can put it with the scrap wood."

They worked in silence for a while, the buzz of the saw and the slam of the hammer music to her ears. "I've decided it's time you hold up your end of the bargain," she said.

"I'm already working my ass off for you."

"No, your list. For what you want in a woman. Have you graduated to date four yet?"

Irritation skittered across his features. She tried to tamp down her delight. "Not yet." She waited him out, learning he liked to space out his responses. "I'm seeing her again this Friday," he added grudgingly.

"Ooh, exciting. Okay, so tell me what floats your boat, Casanova."

He shuddered. "God, please don't call me that. Or talk like that."

"Sorry, I forget you're a bit high class."

"No, I just speak proper English."

"Stop stalling."

He looked away but she caught the edge of a grin. He'd be loath to admit it, but she made him laugh. And from what she'd seen, this man desperately needed someone to balance all that seriousness. It must be exhausting.

"Fine. What do you want to know?"

She practically clapped her hands with glee. "The same question I answered. Tell me the traits in your perfect woman."

His arms flexed as he worked the hammer, and her gaze snagged on the lean, sinewy muscles under gorgeous brown skin. Wood chips and dust clung to his figure but it only added to his attractiveness, giving a sense of ruggedness to his normal poised elegance. Yes, women would definitely seek him out for his appearance alone, but she wondered how many stayed after they got a dose of his attitude. He must be on his best behavior to trick them.

"I don't know why you're interested in this," he muttered.

"Tit for tat."

"It's simple, really. I know exactly what I'm looking for. I'm ready to get married and have a family."

"Right away?"

"Yes. My future wife will have a few core qualities that I won't compromise on. Loyalty, honesty, and dual respect are at the top."

She cocked her head, studying him. He'd managed to surprise her. "Very thoughtful. Excellent choices."

"So glad you approve. I need a certain amount of intellectual stimulation, as I'm sure she will, so she cannot be just a pretty face."

Huh. Maybe she'd been wrong about him. So far, she wholeheartedly agreed with his choices. "Can't argue with those."

"I don't need laugh-out-loud funny, but a sense of humor helps get you through hard times."

"Agreed."

"And then she needs to obey, of course."

The hammer swung. The wood cracked and he began pulling off the remains of the cabinet. She tugged on her earlobe. "I'm sorry. I didn't hear you right. What was the last one?"

"Obey. She has to obey me. I'll be the leader in the relationship, and she'll need to respect my decisions."

She pulled her lobe harder, but her sinking heart confirmed she'd heard correctly. "Did you say the word 'obey'?"

"Yes." He continued, oblivious to her sudden rising body temperature, pounding heart, and slow fist clench. "I'll need to make the proper decisions on finances, but of course, she'll be the primary with the children since she'll be home with them all day."

Her mouth opened and shut like a guppy. "What if she wants to work?"

"Oh, that's not allowed. There will be too much to do running a tight household. Trust me. I've seen the way my mother and sisters handle their time, and you need to be quite organized. Dinner alone takes a chunk out of the day."

Steam began to rise from her head. The room began to sway. "She's going to have dinner ready for you when you come home?"

He grinned. Actually grinned with pleasure. "Of course. There's nothing wrong with understanding and embracing the roles in a marriage. In fact, it's quite a powerful, freeing thing. Society pushes both women and men to do too much crossover, which ends up breaking the relationship at the seams. I won't have that problem in my marriage."

Her voice sounded a few pitches too high when she managed to speak. "But what if you fall in love with a woman who doesn't want to stay home all day with the children and finds fulfillment in her own career?"

He didn't even pause. "Then she's not for me."

The hammer dropped out of her fingers with a crash. He swung his gaze around, frowning. "What's the matter?"

"You're a monster," she whispered. "A chauvinist. A card carrying ego-driven prejudiced male!"

With a long-suffering sigh, he rose to his feet, brushing the dust off his jeans. "Are you going to throw another tantrum because my ideals don't match yours? Who's calling whom chauvinist?"

"You want a Stepford woman. What if she disagrees with you and doesn't think your word is God? What will you do then? Beat her?"

His dark eyes flared with intensity. "If she wants me to," he growled. "Nothing wrong with a good spanking now and then to reset things."

Her stomach dropped at the same time her temper exploded. "My God, you've time traveled from another century and missed the sexual revolution. Women don't obey, Brady. They are equal partners in a relationship."

Irritation bristled from his form. "She will be my equal partner, but she'll respect boundaries and trust I'm making the right decision for all of us."

"That's a dictatorship, not a marriage."

He took a step forward, closing the distance between them. "Hey, just because you're too scared to fully trust and surrender to another person, don't judge me. There's power in submission."

She snorted. "For you, maybe. What about her? Sounds like she has no say in anything, and that, buddy boy, is a foundation for a very unhealthy marriage."

"Did you just call me Buddy Boy?"

She ignored his softly spoken warning, caught in sheer outrage for his future dates. "How early do you let your dates know what you're really looking for? Do you try and seduce them first, then get them to agree? Do you play some Jedi mind tricks on them like on *The Bachelor*, to make them think they need to marry you at all costs? Does this woman you're approaching a fourth date with know what she's getting into?"

He leaned in, toe to toe with her. Her nostrils filled with his scent, a delicious musk reminding her of smoke and sex. He wasn't particularly tall, but his solid, muscular build seethed with leashed power, making shivers trickle down her spine. His coal eyes held a savage gleam, and in that one moment, he seemed almost primeval. The air thickened with a low hum of electricity, as if preparing for a storm. She wanted to spurt more outraged accusations, but his gaze pinned her with a ruthless determination that suddenly made the breath whoosh from her lungs. Her breasts got achy and tight. A low throb pulsed between her legs.

What was going on?

He was pumping out sexual, dominant vibes she'd never caught before. He was cold. Controlled. A bit pompous. A businessman through and through, for goodness sakes. A tad boring. Where had all this hidden intensity come from? And why, oh why was she suddenly weirdly turned on?

"I only sleep with women who know exactly what I want and how I want it. I make sure there's plenty of communication and agreement on both sides before moving forward. There have never been complaints and I expect none in the future." A wolfish smile twisted his sensual lips. "Did you ever stop to wonder what it would feel like to let go of all that control, even for one night? Don't you get tired of trying to do it all when so much pleasure is waiting for you on the other side?"

Oh, hell no. He wasn't going to play her with those dark Latin eyes and hot body. She knew exactly what he was doing, and he'd be the last man on Earth she'd ever fall for. Ignoring her achy body, she rallied and fought back. Lifting her chin, she met his gaze head on. "Oh, don't worry about me. I get plenty of pleasure without having to give up my independence and soul for an orgasm," she said sweetly.

"Maybe you haven't had the proper orgasm." His gravelly voice caressed her ears, and those inky eyes burned like charcoal. "More specifically, orgasms. If a man is giving you just one, he's plain lazy."

Her heart thundered and her palms dampened. She didn't even like the man but her body was strangely turned on with this hot sexual bantering. "Maybe you haven't been introduced to the cutting edge technology they have available that removes a man from the equation," she challenged. "My standards are already high. And multiples are already assumed."

Irritation flickered over his features, along with another emotion she didn't want to name. He moved a step closer. "You're a bona fide brat who needs a bit of taming."

"I'm not starring in *The Taming of the Shrew*. I still think that is the most sexist play ever created. Just tell me this. Does your date know exactly what's expected of her yet, or do you keep that as one of your special surprises?"

"Don't judge me, Charlotte, nor the women I spend my time with. At least I own my stuff and don't try to pretend I'm someone I'm not." His gaze raked over her figure. "I bet you still have no idea what type of man will truly satisfy you."

"Who cares? I only know one important thing. It'll never be you!"

They both stared at each other, caught in a powerful surge of energy that rooted her feet to the floor. She should be stomping away from him, but she couldn't seem to look away. He was so close their breath intermingled, their lips inches apart. Perspiration broke out on her skin. Her breath strangled in her lungs. She waited for him to do something, say something, anything to break her out of this trance. He murmured a curse word, jaw clenched, and his hands snagged her upper arms, ready to shake her, and—

"Stop! Stop right there or I'll bash your brains out, asshole!"

Brady jerked back and stuck his hands in the air. Charlie whirled around and found Jackson holding the baseball bat that was supposed to protect her. She smothered a groan. She had to get rid of that thing. Who would've thought it would end up being the ultimate weapon?

"Jackson, it's okay. This is Brady and he works for me."

The boy's eyes were full of suspicion. He didn't lower the bat, his gaze darting back and forth between them. "He was yelling at you. Grabbed you."

"We're coworkers and we fight a lot. I swear, there's nothing to worry about."

Brady kept his silence, hands up, and waited him out. A grudging respect came over her. She bet many men would have wanted to jump in to control the situation, especially with a teen. Brady let him lead. Slowly, Jackson put down the bat, a flush rising to his cheeks. "Sorry, man. I didn't know what was going on."

Brady lowered his hands and nodded. "Actually, that was pretty damn awesome. Just be careful of busting in on a scene that can get violent. Better to call 911 on your cell first before doing anything."

"Uh, oh, did you call 911?" Charlie asked nervously.

"Nah. I should've thought about it. I went on instinct. Heard voices and the door was unlocked. Didn't think about it until I saw the bat by the door."

Brady muttered something under his breath. "I told you to get the deadbolt fixed," he said to her.

She lifted a brow. "I did. You forgot to lock it behind you today."

Jackson gave a half laugh. Brady chose to ignore her quip and walked toward the boy with his hand extended. "Don't think we officially met. Brady."

They shook hands. "Jackson."

"You were the one crashing at this place?"

Jackson stiffened, but Brady was perfectly at ease, which seemed to relax the boy. "Yeah, wanted some time alone. Didn't know anyone was around." He shifted his weight, his hands clenching around the baseball bat. "Charlie said I could come by and check things out. Said she'd be tearing down a wall."

Brady laughed. "Yep. That's probably one of the most satisfying jobs in renovation. You wanna join us? We're ripping it out tomorrow. Today, we're focused on cabinets."

"Cabinets sound boring."

Charlie stepped forward. "Are you kidding me? It's all about creativity. Seeing what's not there yet and how you can make it different. It's the only time you harness power through your own vision. Come see."

Her tone brooked no argument. Jackson followed her in the kitchen, and she pointed out the half-ripped-out lower cabinets and the guts of plumbing, rotted wood, and empty space. "A good renovator takes this ugliness and sees something bigger. What do you see?"

He stared at her for a while before taking in the scene. "I see a mess."

"Wanna know what I see?"

"What?"

She smiled and floated around the cramped, clutter-filled space. "Right here are beautiful distressed wood cabinets that give off a touch of an older farmhouse look. Think deep sinks, faded-type wood, rustic. Instead of fancy, modern granite, we'll put in lighter wood counters for contrast, all from scrap wood. I'll show you how to make it shine like a deeper grain by using coconut oil."

"No shit?"

"No shit! Umm, does your mom let you curse? Probably not cool at your age. Girls don't like when boys curse a lot either."

"She doesn't like it too much either."

"Okay, so we won't curse. Now, for the top cabinets, I'm going to strip off that crappy green—is crappy a curse word?"

"Don't think so."

"Crappy green and see what I can salvage. I think it would be cool to have the upper and lower cabinets not match. I'm thinking rustic wood on the bottom and white on top."

Brady interrupted. "That sounds like a horror show."

"My mom likes when things match," Jackson said with a touch of worry. "I think most people do."

She wrinkled her nose. "Yeah, but I swear I can pull this off. If I make it homey but with a bit of an edge, I think a family will fall in love with the house because it is different. Who wants a cookie-cutter house? Sometimes it's like food. In your mind, certain ingredients don't go together, but then when the flavors explode on your tongue, it makes sense."

"True." He nodded, squinting a bit as he took in the kitchen. "I still can't really see it."

"Takes a lot of practice. I'll show you the steps if you can make it here after school. But no pressure, just come when you want."

"Cool. Thanks." He turned to Brady, still regarding him with a touch of suspicion. "Will you be here, too?"

"Yeah, I'm not crazy about Charlie working in this neighborhood alone, plus I like to renovate sometimes. I'm usually just an architect."

"You draw buildings and stuff?"

"Yep. And houses and additions and rooms. Anything that's wanted."

Jackson nodded. "Can I hang out and watch a little bit? Or will I be in the way?"

Brady grinned. "Grab a pair of work gloves and help me haul out some of this wood to the scrap pile. I'll show you some more stuff."

"Awesome!"

He dove into the project, and for the next hour, they worked together in a happy comradery. Brady watched him with attentiveness, but after a while, he seemed to realize Jackson was a good kid and had an honest desire to learn. By the time the cabinets were pulled out and she'd selected the pieces she wanted to restore, they were tired and bonded by good, old-fashioned sweat and hard work.

"I better get home," Jackson said with a touch of reluctance. "Mom should be back from work soon. Thanks for letting me help."

"Come back tomorrow and I'll let you smash a bit of the wall," she said brightly.

"Thanks. Bye, Charlie. Bye, Brady!"

He took off with the enthusiasm of youth and disappeared out the door. Brady closed it and clicked the deadbolt firmly into place. She fought a shiver, not wanting to think of their intimate scene before. They had gotten a bit riled up and emotions had turned physical. Simple to explain away, but she wanted no awkwardness between them. Thank God nothing had happened they couldn't come back from. But it seemed Brady had a different opinion. He walked over to her, standing a few inches away, arms crossed in front of his powerful chest, his sooty gaze locked with hers. "Seems like a good kid." He paused. "You're good with kids."

She swallowed, trying to sound light and cheerful. "Thanks. Kids are real. I can deal with real."

"Gotta admit you surprised me a bit today."

"Because I don't hate kids?"

A grin tugged at his full lips. "No. Because you're not flighty, as I originally thought."

She rolled her eyes. "Gee, thanks. But I still think you're a tightass."

"Maybe I have some time to change your mind," he said softly. His voice stroked some hidden parts deep inside—girly parts—that had never been ruffled before. She shifted her weight, nervously nibbling on her thumbnail.

"Umm, Brady—"

"Can I ask you a question?"

Damn. Things were getting out of hand, and she'd have to delicately tell him there was no way in hell anything would ever happen between them. He'd earned her respect by helping her and being cool with Jackson, but after his little speech today about what he wanted from a woman, it was evident they were universes apart. Even with the odd pull of sexual chemistry. "Well, see, I don't think—"

"Are you really going to do white cabinets with rustic wood together? Because I think that's going to be a deal breaker with people. You need to take some time to think about it."

As his words registered, there was only one thing left to do.

She laughed. He grinned back at her, and the last bit of awkwardness and tension drained away. "You just wait, Heart. I'm going to blow your mind when this house is done."

"Never said you weren't going to. Just worried in what capacity it'll be. Come on. Let's get out of here and call it a night."

They packed up their tools and headed out. He was becoming a better renovation partner than she'd originally thought.

Chapter Eight

"Whatever good things we build end up building us."—Jim Rohn

"What are you doing here?"

Charlie grinned as Dalton stepped over the debris, his sharp gaze traveling over the house. As a master woodworker, Dalton had been the one who suggested she start working at Pierce Brothers. One soul recognized the other. They were both madly in love with renovation and woodworking and had formed a tight bond over the past months.

"Checking up on you since I was in the area. Where's Brady?"

She tilted her head and gave him a look. "Dude, really? You checking to see if I have my babysitter? He should be here soon."

"Partner," he corrected. "Assistant. Not caretaker. And I'm checking to see if you need anything from me and how it's progressed. Taking down the wall today?"

"Yep. Getting there slow and steady. Hey, do you happen to have an extra circular saw I can use?"

"Of course. I'll bring it tomorrow. This is an exciting canvas. Whatcha doing with woodwork?"

She rubbed her hands together with glee and motioned him toward the kitchen. "Taking the windows and building an extra cabinet for storage space. Gonna build my own countertops and do a mismatch of cabinets."

He nodded slowly, interest piquing in his blue eyes. "Gutsy, but I like it. Let me know if you need an extra set of hands sometime. Be happy to help."

Her heart softened. She might have been pissed over the Pierces' overprotectiveness, but there was also a sense of family and shelter she loved. "Thanks. I'll let you know."

"How are you getting along with Brady?"

She regarded Dalton with curiosity. "We're managing."

Dalton gave a short laugh. "I know you two haven't been close in the past, but I was hoping this project would help bring you together."

She narrowed her gaze. "What do you mean?"

"What I said. It's easier if we all get along at the office, right?"

She relaxed. He had no ulterior motives. She was just being completely paranoid. They'd shared a small, tiny moment together, which meant nothing. It had all been based on annoyance and temper. "Right. So, you and Brady have known each other a long time, huh?"

Dalton walked through the rooms, studying the layout. "Yep. He met Cal in college and became almost like an adopted brother. He remained solid even during our period of hating one another. Never took a side—he was just there for all of us."

She wasn't surprised. Brady was loyal; that much was evident. "What about his family? I asked him about his background because his name was English and not Latino."

Dalton laughed. "Oh, don't mention the name thing. That's a hot spot with him. I only use his birth name when I want to seriously piss him off."

"What is it?"

"Can't tell you. He'll castrate me, and don't think I'm joking."

Damn, now she really had to know. She was very good at getting her answers, so she launched into the famous diversion attack. Her mother had always told her she'd be deadly in a courtroom if she ever wanted to be a lawyer. "Fine. Is he close with his family? What are they like?"

"He eats dinner with them every other Sunday. The other times he's at our house. They're awesome. His mom makes fabulous dinners, and his sisters really look up to Brady. They're a tight-knit crew, but very traditional."

Ah, ha. "Traditional how?" she asked casually.

He examined the moldings, running his fingers over the inside windows, and seemingly calculating distance and ideas in his head. "Are these the windows you're using as cabinets?"

"Yes."

"Interesting. Can't wait to see the finished product."

"How is his family traditional?"

"Oh, his sisters both defer to their husbands, just like his mom. Guess the men in the family are raised to be the leaders. The women all stay at home to take care of the kids and run the household."

"You don't think that's a bit archaic?"

He shrugged. "I guess. It works for them, and they're pretty damn happy. Who are we to judge what's right or wrong for anyone based on societal expectations?"

She jerked back. The words hit her like a sucker punch, and a sense of shame trickled through her. She'd never really thought of it like that. She'd been so outraged at the idea, she didn't stop to think whether it was forced on women or freely chosen. In a way, she was being a reverse chauvinist. "I guess you're right. I'm sure there's plenty of ways his sisters can get what they want. Like his real name. If they know how much he hates it, I bet they've tortured him over that a few times."

Dalton laughed. "Yeah, I'll never forget that one time his sister Cecilia snuck out to date this boy, and he was yelling at her, acting all manly, and she just shouted his name in front of her date: 'You're not my papa, Bolivar!' and his date was like, 'What's your brother's name?' and Brady got all embarrassed and—"

Dalton trailed off. Slowly, horror leaked over his features, and he slapped his hand over his mouth.

Charlie's eyes widened. "His name is Bolivar?"

"Shit. Ah, shit! I swear, Charlie, I will kill you if you repeat that to him. No one is supposed to know."

Actually, she loved the name. It was formal and regal and full of pride. But knowing she had the secret weapon, like Rumpelstiltskin, gave her a rush of adrenaline. Oh, the ways she could use this to her advantage. She kept her tone sugary sweet. "Don't worry. I promise I won't tell."

He opened his mouth to say something but the door interrupted him. Brady stepped through, grinning in welcome. "Hey, dude.

What's up? Am I needed at the office?"

Shooting her a warning glare, Dalton cleared his throat and walked toward him. "Nah, just checking in. Wanted to see the house and the progress. Looks great."

"Charlie's doing a good job." His words came out true and clear, and a thrill of pleasure caught her unaware. Seemed his opinion meant more than she had originally thought. "Hey, can we borrow your extra circular saw? We need to do some cabinet work."

Dalton raised a brow. "Yeah, I told Charlie I'd drop it off tomorrow." He shot them both a weird look, then shook his head. "Gotta head out. I have a dining room table that's overdue for a client. See you guys later."

They said their good-byes. Silence enveloped the room. She averted her gaze, afraid her face would give away the sheer glee of knowing his secret name. "Haven't seen Jackson yet, so maybe we should get started. But don't feel you need to stay with me the whole time. There hasn't been any trouble or people bothering me, and I think we both know it's completely safe here."

"What are you hiding?"

Her mouth fell open. She quickly shut it. "What are you talking about? I'm not hiding anything."

His narrowed gaze raked over her figure, probing way too deep. Holy hell, why couldn't she be a better liar? "No. You're holding something back. And frankly, it terrifies me."

Surprise flickered through her. "You? Terrified? Not of a woman who's only here to listen to your instructions and do as she's told?"

The moment the words came out, she regretted them. Especially after seeing the flash of hurt on his face before it was replaced by cold dismissal. "Think what you want. Let's concentrate on work." He grabbed the hammer, donned gloves, and began setting up.

She watched him in misery for a while. "Brady?"

"Yeah?"

"I'm sorry."

His shoulders stiffened. He didn't turn back around. "Forget it."

"No, I really am sorry. Listen, I may not agree with your outlook, but there are plenty of relationships that work well. Who am I to judge you or what makes you happy? I'm kind of ashamed I gave you such a hard time. So, I'm offering my apology."

He turned around, met her stare head on, then slowly nodded. "Apology accepted."

Relief flowed through her. She was glad Dalton had stopped in. Of course, she still knew Brady would eventually piss her off again, so having his name as her artillery was exactly what she needed to balance the scales. "Thank you."

The knock on the door interrupted anything further. Brady walked over to open it, motioning Jackson in. "Good to see you. Thought you wouldn't be able to make it today."

"Me either." The boy trudged inside with a gloomy look on his face. She exchanged a glance with Brady, noting the difference immediately. Underneath the normal tough exterior Jackson liked to emanate, he was enthusiastic and excited to learn new things. She genuinely enjoyed his company and sense of humor, liking the way he was able to soften Brady's usual crusty surface and get him to share some real belly laughs. But now? Obviously, something had happened. Shadows clung to his dark eyes.

"You okay?" Brady asked him.

"Sure. What do you want me to do?"

Charlie hesitated. She didn't know Jackson that well and had no idea if it was right to push him to share. She tried to act casual. "Bad day at school?"

He didn't answer. Just shrugged.

Sympathy tugged at her heart. God, school was sometimes so brutal. Finding your way, finding yourself, staying sane. She wished she could save children the heartache of growing up and dealing with peers, but it was part of the journey and built the fortitude needed to live life fully.

Still, it just plain sucked.

"Jackson, do you know how each job has something in it that is the best part?" Brady asked.

The boy shook his head. "Like what?"

"Like if you're a writer, the best part is working in your pajamas all day. If you own a bakery, the best part is sampling all the yummy treats."

A ghost of a smile skirted Jackson's lips. "I get it. The best part about being a teacher is summer vacations."

"Exactly!" Brady handed him a protective glass mask, smock, and a hammer. "This is the best part of renovating a house. You get to smash something into smithereens without worrying about the mess or someone getting mad."

Charlie jumped right in. "Brady's right. When I get to take down walls, I imagine everything that frustrates me, makes me mad, makes me sad, and then I let it rip. Let's show you first how it's done, and then we'll let you take your whacks."

The brightness ignited in his dark eyes. They donned their protective gear and tools and stood in front of the wall. "Step back, Jackson."

He obeyed, stopping a safe distance away. Charlie looked at Brady and nodded. In sync, they arced the sledgehammers over their heads and hit the wall together in coordinated efficiency.

With a satisfying crack, plaster exploded. The hole was large, but there was more to be done. Charlie funneled all her energy into attacking the wall until there was a decent space in the middle. She motioned Jackson over. "Okay, stand with your feet braced apart. This hammer is heavy so be careful and watch your range. You want a smooth, full arc as you hit it. Don't forget to summon all that junk inside and let it out with the hammer. Ready?"

His voice shook slightly with excitement. "Ready."

He swung the hammer with little expertise and a lot of enthusiasm. The wall splintered and widened the space. He shot her a delighted grin and waited.

She grinned back. "Again."

Jackson hammered the wall under her supervision while Brady helped and pointed out tips along the way. By the time the debris littered the wood floors, and the kitchen now shone brightly through, no longer masked, she felt a bit lighter. From the dazed look on Jackson's face, she immediately recognized a fellow soul.

He loved it.

"That. Was. Awesome," he said. "What next?"

"Cleaning it up. See what a difference it makes in the layout of the house? More open and accessible."

He studied the new space, slowly nodding. "Yeah, I get it now. But I'm still not sure about those weird cabinets."

Brady laughed. "Agreed. We may need to pull her back from the abyss of bad taste, Jackson."

She shot them both a mock glare. "With you as partners, who needs enemies?"

Brady and Jackson shared a high-five.

They spent the rest of their time carting pieces of the wall to the dumpster and exposing the last of the beams. By the time Jackson was ready to go home, his step was lighter and his face had smoothed out to the carefree youthful expression she hoped he wore more often. His teeth flashed white in a wide grin as he rushed out.

Brady shook his head. "That was the best medicine for him today. Middle school is a nightmare."

She shuddered. "You're telling me. I was always being made fun of because of my clothes and my uncoolness."

Surprise flickered in his dark eyes. "You? Funny, I pegged you for the bubbly cheerleader type with a whole bunch of friends."

"Oh, Lord, no. My mom and I moved a lot, always trying to get cheaper rent, and I was so damn poor my clothes were bargain basement. You know how kids like the designer brand? Let's just say mine was the no-name brand."

"You were poor?"

She swept the floor with a broom, catching the last of the remnants. "Yep. We lived in a motel at certain times. Thank goodness for the backpack program and the food pantry to help us when things were really bad. But eventually, Mom got a decent job and we had an apartment and a car. But kids can be mean. I never really fit in, even though I finally made some friends."

He didn't speak for a while, but the silence felt comfortable. She continued sweeping. His voice deepened, rising to her ears like seductive smoke. "Is that why you're always looking to save money?"

She threw back her head and laughed. "Hell, yes. That's why I'm cheap. Frugal. Call it whatever you want. It's embedded in my DNA. I get off on saving money for some reason. There's such a waste in society today, it hurts my heart. People throw things away without seeing their real value. That's exactly what I love about a renovation project rather than a new build."

"What about your dad?"

His tone was soft and respectful. She paused in her sweeping and smiled. "Never knew him. Never missed him either. My mom is pretty great. She can fix anything, from a broken car engine to a faulty pipe. You know what I think?"

"What?"

"I think if we weren't poor and got to buy stuff, I would've never discovered I had a gift for renovation. Maybe I would've taken it for granted. I'm glad I found my passion in life while so many others drift by, looking for something more to fulfill them. Does that make sense?"

His gaze dove deep, saw everything, and stayed anyway. "Yeah. It makes perfect sense."

The silence shifted, grew, simmered. Suddenly uneasy, she swallowed and took a casual step back. There it was again. That change of consciousness, as if the universe was forcing them to see something neither of them wanted. Her skin prickled in response, and the scent of musk and virile sweaty male filled the air, pumping in waves around her.

She ripped her gaze away and propped the broom back in the closet. Her heart pounded so hard she swore he heard it. What was happening between them lately? Why was she suddenly so aware of him? She cleared her throat. "Sounds corny, right?" she forced out. "Like tricking your mind to believe the bad stuff is really good. Guess you'd call it juvenile."

"Don't." His voice was a whiplash, stilling her back into silence. He crossed the room and stood before her. Slowly, he reached out and tipped her chin up. A slight frown creased his brow, the expression he usually wore when confronted by a stubborn project or when she was driving him nuts with her banter. Only this time, his dark eyes seethed with raw emotion. "It's not corny. It's not juvenile. It's brave and good and damn humbling. I was wrong about you."

Her eyes widened. His finger on her skin burned, causing a rush of heat to pool and pound mercilessly between her thighs. "How?"

A muscle ticked in his jaw. "I judged you. Thought you came from a cushy background. Thought you were dabbling in renovation because you were bored. Thought you were reckless and silly."

The words hurt, but she met his gaze head on, sensing a shift between them. "What do you think now?" she asked softly.

"I think every day you amaze me a little bit more, Charlotte Grayson."

A tiny gasp escaped her lips. A surging sexual chemistry took them in a tight hold, and they stared at one another for seconds, minutes, centuries. He was so close his scent surrounded her with rich cloves, and her hands ached to drag him forward and feel those lips over hers just once.

Just once...

Instead, panic tore through her and she stumbled back, breaking the connection. Instantly, a shutter slammed over his face, and the sexual tension fizzled like a bottle of seltzer going immediately flat. Confusion swamped her. The jagged seesaw of emotion between them was too overwhelming. This was a man she worked with. A man who had completely different philosophies on relationships. A man who frustrated her on a constant basis.

This was one time in her life she could not afford to be impulsive.

"I'd better get going," she said. Her voice was a bit too high, but he followed her lead and turned away.

"Sure. I'll walk you out."

She didn't even get mad anymore at his insistence to accompany her everywhere. She'd gotten used to the protectiveness he afforded her. Lately, he seemed less domineering and more...sweet. He refused to leave the site without her safely in her truck, driving away. Once, she caught him behind her following her to her house. She'd parked, jumped out to yell at him, but he just sped past without a second glance. The man was pure stubbornness.

Like her.

Boy, they'd be a disaster together. They grabbed their stuff and locked up, walking to the car. Freaked out by the awkward silence, she burst out with the first question she could think of. "Have a date tonight?"

He stiffened. For one moment, she wondered if she'd glimpsed hurt in his eyes, but it disappeared so quickly she knew she imagined it. "No."

Instead of getting in her damn car, she kept making it worse, not able to silence her mouth. "Is she still on the hook or did you scare her away?"

The more familiar expression of irritation was back on his face. Thank goodness. Much more comfortable this way. She squashed the tiny flicker of regret, refusing to think about it. "We're seeing each other this weekend."

"Good. Really good. Does she seem like the type of woman you want?"

His gaze raked over her, probing in the darkness for something she couldn't name. Didn't want to name. He paused. "She seems...perfect."

She ignored the sharp pang that struck her. She was glad he'd found someone who was more of a match for him. Hell, the pang was probably envy he'd found the ONE. Who wouldn't be? Sure, she wasn't ready to settle down like he was or have kids, but didn't everyone dream about finding a soul mate? "That's great! Really, really, great." Ugh, why was her voice so high and fake? She was tired. She had to get out of here. "See you tomorrow."

He regarded her for a few moments while she held her breath. Then he nodded and turned away. "'Night."

She got in her car and drove away, wondering why her heart ached.

Chapter Nine

"Excuses are the nails used to build a house of failure."—Don Wilder

He was in a piss-poor mood.

Brady brooded as he watched her animatedly tutor Jackson in the art of flipping a window frame into a cabinet. The new windows were propped up, ready for installation, with a nice thick layer to insulate the house. The woman had gone on a hunt for the best deal, calling in favors and negotiating like it was a used car. She finally scored a bargain basement deal because Bakers Glass Warehouse had gotten tired of dealing with her.

She was the definition of persistence.

Sitting cross-legged on a blanket, she chipped away at the layers of cheap paint, an arsenal of products lined up to help her transform something old to something new.

Personally, he didn't think she'd be able to do it, but that's not what bothered him. No, it was much deeper than that. The woman was beginning to affect his personal life on a grand scale, and if he didn't get a handle on it, things were going to explode.

Marissa wanted to sleep with him. It was obvious from their last dinner together. She needed no further courting. They'd gone way past the third and fourth date in the last few weeks, and he sensed the beginning of her frustration. The good-night kiss and tame foreplay had reached an end. She was ready to take the next step, and so was he. The problem was more serious than he'd originally thought.

His dick just refused to respond.

No matter how hard he tried, he couldn't get excited about bringing her to his bed.

Because all he could think about was Charlie.

Brady smothered a groan and concentrated on his task. The thick humidity had finally drifted away with the end of summer, and a gorgeous late September breeze blew in like a gentle lover's kiss. Fall hovered, tempting the northeast with eye-popping colors as the leaves turned and the earth was drenched in golden light. It was his favorite time of year, and the height of the building season.

They'd been working together nonstop for the last two months and had found their rhythm. Though they still bantered and insulted, it had a softened edge. Respect had grown out of cramped quarters. And something more. Something dangerous.

It had been two weeks since their last encounter when he'd almost kissed her. That almost kiss haunted him on a daily basis. That almost kiss had caused a shift between them, igniting a sensual awareness that was with them every moment of every day. They both ignored the simmering attraction and stuck to business, but it was getting harder and harder to pretend he didn't want her.

"Hey, Brady, Jackson said next Friday his mom has a work thing so I thought we'd throw a pizza party here. If you don't have a date with Marissa, how about joining us?" she called out.

Jackson hooted. "Is she hot?"

He straightened his shoulders. "Of course. She's with me, isn't she?"

Charlie grinned and shook her head. Ash- and timber-colored strands of hair brushed her shoulders and clung to her cheek. "Egomaniac. She's only with you for the free dinners, dude."

Jackson thought that was hysterical, bringing a reluctant grin to Brady's lips. Somehow, they'd created a bit of a ragtag crew of three, all with one focus: restore the house so it could live again. Before, Charlie's chaotic work process had struck him as sloppy and disrespectful. Now, he saw how her vision of a house was so pure, she'd do anything to keep it. The work was part of her makeup and soul, striking him a bit like Dalton when he worked on a piece of wood. Brady had always respected that quality, even as he bemoaned the sometimes ragged timeline that screwed things up for him.

It was a different way of looking at things, and he was getting better at seeing the bigger picture. He'd gained a deep respect for her as a professional and a woman who'd overcome a challenging past to make herself better.

Too bad he still wanted to strip her clothes, part her thighs, and make her scream with pleasure.

"Earth to Brady. Next Friday good?"

"Sure."

She frowned, as if noticing his response was lackluster. "Come over here."

"Busy now. Later." Hell, he was sporting wood on a whole new level just by the image of Charlie naked. Marissa was beautiful and sweet. Her dark hair and eyes bespoke a Latina heritage he loved. She was soft spoken and never argued with him. She wanted a family immediately. She knew his parents through the church. She also gave plenty of indication she'd be open minded in the bedroom, which was a must.

Then why hadn't he taken her yet? Why wasn't it her naked form he was currently visualizing in his head?

Because he couldn't get Charlotte out of his damn head.

He slammed the window in, causing a loud shriek of protest from the shrinking wood. "Hey, be careful with my windows!" she shouted out. "Do you need help?"

He gritted his teeth. "I got it."

"Doesn't look like you got it."

"I got it, okay!" He shoved. With a weak protest, the frame slid in. "See?"

"I'll do the other one. I have a gentler approach."

"Stop being a control freak and paint your damn window cupboard DIY project!"

Jackson winced. "Umm, Brady, do you need to smash a wall or something? Bad day?"

Charlie slapped her hand over her mouth but not before a giggle burst through. With his dick hard, his hands smarting, and his heart confused, he glared at both of them, then stormed out. "I need a break. Gonna get some air."

He sat on the broken stoop and guzzled water, calming himself. Enough. He was going to fuck Marissa's brains out and he was going to love it. They were already falling in love. They'd get married in church, have beautiful babies, and she'd be the perfect wife. Done.

"Do you want to take off?"

Her soft voice stroked his ears and he half closed his eyes, wishing she'd go away. "No. Just want to drink my water in peace."

She ignored him, plopping herself beside him. Her wide, thickly lashed eyes were filled with concern. The tangy scent of citrus drifted to his nostrils. He'd discovered she had a weakness for grapefruits in the morning. He'd never imagined the scent could set off pure lust, but he was beginning to realize a whole lot of things lately. "You've been here every day, and it was wrong of me to begin taking you for granted. I don't know how it happened, but I feel like we've built this crew and you both belong to me. Stupid, right? Especially when I was against you even being here and we couldn't stand being in the same room together."

You both belong to me…

His inner caveman roared to life, wondering what it would be like to belong to Charlotte Grayson. He'd feast on her for hours, learning what every moan and whimper meant. He'd tear off those ridiculous clothes and taste and touch every inch of her beautiful body. He'd take her to places she'd dreamed about, and then take her there again and again. He'd fuck her, please her, claim her. A shudder wracked his body as a sudden primal need overtook him. He clenched his fists and breathed slow and deep, harnessing the arousal she didn't even seem to notice.

"But you have a life you've been putting on hold. Why don't you work with me every other day? Jackson has been great. There's no trouble here. Even some neighbors have come over to introduce themselves and say how happy they are to get a nice house to add to the neighborhood."

Damn her. First, she never wanted to even acknowledge the almost kiss. Then she insisted on treating him like some distant work buddy. And now she wanted to completely dismiss him? "We made a deal. I'm sticking to it, and you better do the same."

Her brows snapped together. Much better. He could deal with her when she was annoyed with him and he with her. Things were clearer that way. "I'm trying to be nice," she explained. "I just don't think I need you anymore."

Hurt lashed at him. Caught off guard, he fired back. "Glad to know I'm so dispensable. But even if you insist on making cupboards out of windows, and pizza art boxes, and ridiculous wall murals in the kitchen like a craft show gone bad, I made a promise to stay until the last damn nail is in. Got it?"

"Just because you're so narrow minded and scared to get outside the box, don't put your crap on me. I never needed you in the first place. You're the liability here! I'm practically carrying you along, so do us both a favor and we'll both tell Cal we're good to part ways."

Adrenaline pumped through his veins. He practically snarled the words in irritation. "Here's a hint. Going outside the box is sometimes not a good thing."

"What do you know? Have you ever been pushed to create something from nothing? I bet your own house is technically beautiful, with all the latest gadgets and a sleek, modern feel. But guess what? I bet it's all empty inside. No surprises. No creativity. And no soul." She spit out her last words in a staccato rhythm that made a smear of red blur his vision.

"Here we go again with the tortured, poor artist you like to bring out when challenged. Coloring inside the lines is not all bad, Charlotte." He sneered her full name with sarcastic intent. Her widened eyes told him it struck home. She'd gotten used to hearing her formal name from him and usually didn't snap back. Maybe she sensed the intention not to mock, but an underlying intimacy they both sensed and accepted.

But this time, his intention was to completely piss her off.

Choppy pants broke from her gumball lips. Hazel eyes blazed with scorching heat. Her body trembled and his responded instantly, unfurling with a crazed need to yank her against him and kiss her the way she should be kissed, by a man and not the boys he bet she dated. He reached out slowly, his logic long gone under the sting of her words and her attitude and her damn delectable mouth, and then—

"It may not be bad, Bolivar," she drawled, "but it's boring as hell."

He froze, staring at her with a growing horror, hoping he heard wrong. The smug arrogance glowing from her features told him he'd gotten it right the first time.

She knew his birth name.

Someone was going to die.

"What did you call me?" he asked softly, a clear warning vibrating from his chest.

She didn't even blink. "Bolivar. Your real name. Kind of cute, actually. All formal and regal. Full of male posturing pride. Not sure why you're so embarrassed by it."

This was not happening. His ears actually got hot, and he prayed they didn't look red. "You will never call me by that again. Do you understand? Who told you?"

She broke into a delighted grin. Why was she never afraid of him? Or even cautious? "No one. I just did my research. Now, you can decide to lose your attitude and come back inside to help or knock off for the rest of the day. I don't really care, *Bolivar*."

He gnashed his teeth together and his hands fisted. He was going to choke her. He was actually going to murder a poor defenseless female, except she was anything but. "I swear to you, Charlotte, if you push me on this you will regret it."

"Okay." She jumped up from the step, dusted off her jeans, which actually boasted pink flowers on the sides, and grinned wider. "Bolivar, Bolivar, Bolivar," she sang in an off-key song.

He got up and reached for her, ready to spank her sweet ass, but she broke into giggles and danced away, his name still falling from her lips.

The door slammed behind her.

Brady closed his eyes and groaned. This was a nightmare. He fucking hated that name. He'd been tortured in school until he declared to the family he'd no longer answer to Bolivar and changed it to Brady. It had taken his parents a while, but he was so crazed and insistent, they finally listened. Even his sisters were afraid to use it.

But not *her*.

Like the damn fairytale, he had a feeling the secret of his real name would be his downfall. She'd torture him endlessly because she acted like a child. A woman child. Who could possibly handle her on a full-time basis?

No one. Including him.

Tempted to walk away, he forced himself to drag in a breath and stand. Best to get back in there and not mention anything. Concentrate on finishing the window work, and he'd cut out early.

He'd squeeze in an impromptu date with Marissa and get his life back on track where it belonged.

He refused to allow Charlotte Grayson to kidnap his heart.

He guzzled the rest of his water and walked back inside.

Chapter Ten

"Creativity requires the courage to let go of certainties."—Erich Fromm

"It's too big. No way will it fit."

His voice was full of impatience. "Of course it'll fit. Just use some more lube and relax. Why do you have to make things so difficult?"

"Me? You're the one who wanted the screw! I told you this whole thing wouldn't work."

He grunted. "Open up, dammit. You're not helping me at all here!"

"I swear, if you hurt me, I'll pepper spray you again!"

His hands clenched. Sweat dotted his brow. "I won't hurt you. Just relax. I'm going in, okay?"

"Fine, just do it!"

He pushed through the resistance and finally the cabinet slid in with a pop. Shaking out her fingers, she examined the frame for damage, noticing the wood hadn't cracked and everything fit perfectly. She'd argued against using the extra screws but Brady insisted it would be more stable. Guess he'd been right, even though she'd hate to admit it.

He puffed up his chest in macho pride. "See? Told you we just needed more lube."

An amused, masculine voice cut through the tension-filled air.

"Damn, that was hot. Am I interrupting something?"

Charlie jumped and swung around. Gage stood in the doorway, a huge grin plastered on his face. As usual, he wore nerdy white sneakers, old jeans, and a ripped Metallica concert T-shirt. His hair was mussed under his red baseball hat, and his jaw unshaven. He looked like he'd gone on a bender for a few nights, but Charlie knew it was part of his usual messy demeanor.

"Gage!" With a delighted laugh, she threw herself across the room for a quick hug. "What are you doing here?"

"Wanted to see how you were managing your difficult new lover."

Brady cleared his throat. "Umm, we're not lovers. Just work partners." His voice held a clip of annoyance, as if he hated the idea of them being linked. Charlie ignored the flash of hurt that caught her on the chin like a sucker punch. Damn, he still didn't think much of her, even after all this time. Had it been childish to hope these past months had bonded them? Maybe it was all in her head. Maybe he still looked at her as a chore and thought her ideas were juvenile. Her heart squeezed, but she fought past it, pissed that she still cared.

"He's talking about the house," she retorted.

"She looks at houses as men," Gage explained. "Kind of a weird love-affair thing to me, but damn, girl, you done good. He's looking great."

She beamed up at him. "Thanks! I told you I'd make you proud."

"You always do." He tugged on her hair with affection, then walked across the room, holding out his hand. "Gage Masterson. I sold Charlie the house."

Brady nodded, reaching out to shake his hand. "Brady Heart. I'm with Pierce Brothers. Helping her with the renovation."

"Nice. Finally took my advice and asked for some help, huh?"

She snorted at the same time Brady did. "Hardly," she muttered. "Let's say they insisted on providing me with a helper, whether or not I wanted one."

Gage frowned. "Why are you so damn stubborn? There's nothing wrong with needing help. Especially with a bastard like this."

"What did you say?" Brady asked.

Gage grinned and pointed to the ceiling. "Sorry. I meant the house. Charlie has me thinking about them in male terms and it's damn annoying. Wanna show me the rest of your place?"

"Yes, come with me and I'll give you the full tour." Without another glance, she ignored Brady and grabbed Gage's hand, tugging him out of the kitchen. "Let's start in the basement."

Son of a bitch.

Who the hell was this guy?

Brady fumed at her careless dismissal and began cleaning up. She'd told him before she wasn't dating anyone. He'd figured all her time was spent on the house or at Pierce Brothers, so it'd be hard to find someone new for a while. But if he'd sold her this house, maybe they'd been dating all along? The guy seemed nice enough, but a bit scruffy around the edges. Is that what she preferred?

The fact throbbed under his skin like a splinter. He'd never seen him around before, though, and she didn't mention him. Maybe it was a strictly casual relationship? Or a once in a while hookup? And why the hell did he care?

He shook his head, reaching for patience. Probably because he'd been unable to close the deal with Marissa. She'd gone away to visit her family for two weeks, so their next date had been postponed. He needed to stop worrying about who Charlie dated and concentrate on finishing up this damn house and moving on.

Trying to keep his focus, he cleaned up, his gaze taking in what Gage had seen for the first time. Like a child who had grown up before his eyes, he realized he hadn't noticed how well it was shaping up.

The new windows and floors gave off more space and light, and with the wall gone, the house had a flow it had been missing before. The disastrous kitchen was slowly taking shape. Charlie had stuck to her plan, rebuilding the cabinets in different forms for the upper and lower. They weren't painted, and the counters weren't installed, and the window frame they'd just shoved in to build a half pantry was unfinished, but he was able to spot the full vision. He couldn't believe it, but it was possible she'd pull it off. Of course, he couldn't imagine what type of mural anyone would want in their kitchen, but maybe he could talk her out of that. They still had the roof to replace, and the porch, but the main renovation was behind them. She'd even managed to find matching shingles and only had to replace a quarter of the outside.

Gage's voice floated up the stairs, blending with Charlie's musical laugh. Wind chimes. Why did her voice remind him of the happy quality of bells tinkling in the breeze?

"You're on," she said, entering the kitchen. "It's been way too long and it's already late."

"Done. We'll grab a bite there." Gage turned and shot him a look. "Hey, Brady. Wanna join us?"

"Where?"

"Heading to the restaurant and dance club Tangos. They have salsa dancing Thursday nights."

Charlie waved her hand in the air. "Brady doesn't dance."

"I'd love to come."

It was worth it to see her mouth open. Was she angry he was interrupting her alone time with Gage? Or did she even care? He probed her gaze but was only able to spot pure surprise. Satisfaction ran through him. Good. About time he threw her off balance.

"Great," Gage said. "Do you know where the place is? I'll meet you there in an hour or so? Just gonna head home and change."

"Sounds good," he said. "I'll be there."

With a frown, Charlie walked him to the door, then came back. Her teeth nibbled on her lower lip. "Umm, Brady? You don't have to go if you don't want to. Tangos may be a bit out of your league. The restaurant is small and it only serves tapas. The music is really loud and most people who go are there to dance. I don't think you'll feel comfortable."

Anticipation thickened his blood. He grinned real slow. "Don't worry about me, Charlotte. I can handle it. But I appreciate the heads-up. Now, let's get packed up and call it a day so I can go change."

Still nibbling on her lip, she nodded, but her greenish-brown eyes were filled with doubt.

Oh, he was really looking forward to this.

Chapter Eleven

"If opportunity doesn't knock, build a door."—Milton Berle

Charlie squeezed herself between Gage and Brady at the packed bar and ordered a Blue Moon. The upbeat music of trumpets and clave filled the air, revving up the crowd. Gage pushed a twenty dollar bill onto the bar, handing Brady his IPA, and motioned them toward a corner where they could take in the atmosphere and lean comfortably. Gage hooked his fingers through hers, making sure she wasn't bumped or jostled, and she fought a smile. Too bad Tom couldn't come tonight. He was stuck working late again at the restaurant, which was another reason Gage had been insistent on a night out. She loved taking turns dancing with both of them at the club, even though most assumed they were part of a ménage. At least, that's what she told herself as the reason men never hit on her here.

Brady shot her a cool look at their clasped hands, then glanced away. Her skin prickled with awareness. Ever since they'd left the house, she hadn't been able to rationalize the tension in the air. It was almost as if he was bothered by the idea of her and Gage being a couple. She hadn't told him about Tom—it was none of his business and Gage's call. But if he did believe they were together, why would he possibly care?

The image of that almost kiss slammed into her vision. She'd spent the last weeks burying the memory far underground, desperate to ignore the awareness between them. Instead, every day drove her a bit more mad.

His fingers sliding over hers when they adjusted a cabinet. The stretch of his jeans over that tight ass as he bent over. The dark, velvety pull of those sooty eyes as he gazed at her in moody silence, as if thinking things he didn't want her to know.

Bad things.

She shivered and pressed closer to Gage. Gage drummed his fingers on her hip to the music, content to watch the crowd and drink his own beer. She snuck a sideways glance at Brady, still surprised he'd actually shown up. Even more surprising was his comfort level. She'd expected him to be overdressed, uptight, and a bit awkward.

Instead, he seemed to fit right in.

His jeans were dark-washed and snug. His charcoal button-down shirt had a fancy navy scroll at the cuffs and neck, but looked amazing with his dark hair and eyes. His shoes were red Italian leather that was probably ridiculously expensive and impossible to dance in, but again, they looked good on him. He cocked out his hip, beer casually hooked from his fingers as he took in the dancers. His scent drifted from his skin in an intoxicating flavor of spice and sea salt, reminding her of the special caramels she ordered by the box and only devoured on Valentine's Day for her own special present to herself.

Not that she wanted to devour him.

Absolutely not.

She shifted her weight closer to Gage and surveyed the room. Tangos reminded her of those old jazz bars where people jammed together at too tiny tables to hear great music. It was hidden underground, with only one half-lit neon sign to advertise its presence. This was a club that wasn't on Facebook or heavily marketed, because the true fans of Latin music poured in on a regular basis. All forms of dance were highlighted, but salsa was the most favored. Here, the club demanded participation and took their dancing seriously. The darkness lent an air of mystery, and the pounding, energized music lent an air of sexuality. Bodies twisted together on the dance floor, highlighted by flashing red lights, squeezed tight yet claiming their own space by the demands of each couple. The air hung heavy with the ripe scents of sweat and skin, with alcohol and musk, with pungent arousal. The bar was separated from the dance floor by a low wall, and the dining area consisted of small round tables and wooden chairs jammed into every available space. Exposed brick walls collided with red accents, leading to an open floor area packed with dancers.

She'd taken salsa lessons a few years ago and fell in love with the fast, fluid moves that demanded skill, enthusiasm, and high energy.

Gage ducked his head to whisper in her ear. "Ready to dance?"

"Sure." She turned to Brady, speaking directly in his ear. "Gage and I are hitting the floor. Will you be okay alone?"

She expected him to make an excuse to leave, but he only nodded, those dark eyes filled with a mixture of emotions she couldn't name. "Go ahead, have fun."

She forced a smile. "Thanks." Then she allowed Gage to lead her onto the floor.

When she looked back, Brady had been swallowed up by the crowd. She worried if a woman asked him to dance, he'd panic, but then she was on the floor and the only thing that demanded her attention was the music. Half closing her eyes, she began to soften and relax, to embrace the music and release all the tension she carried with her, shedding her body of expectations and responsibilities and the cares of life.

Her feet spun, tapped, glided. Gage was a solid partner, holding her hands in a firm grip, yet allowing her to lead slightly since he knew she always enjoyed a say in the steps. Her hips swayed, her back arched, and she let herself go free.

God, she loved dancing.

Poor Brady. He had no idea what he was missing.

Brady watched her out on the floor, his gaze pinned to every movement of her body. God, she was gorgeous. He'd never seen someone so enthralled with the music, so able to surrender to the inner demands of the physical and emotional entwined together. Dancing the salsa required a delicate balance, a merging of release and precision, of control and surrender, and if done correctly, the outcome was pure ecstasy—almost orgasmic.

She had no clue he'd been raised on salsa dancing. The tango.

The merengue. He'd been taught to embrace all Latin dances since his parents had been regularly dancing since he was a child. He'd actually been to Tangos a few times but had never seen Charlie or Gage here before.

She danced the salsa like she'd been born to it. Limbs loose and elegant, arms holding a firm frame to Gage, her hips rolled and her feet flashed as she spun to the jungle beat of the trumpets and horns and clave, the music encouraging the dancers to go deeper, get wild, lose themselves in the energy of the moment.

He'd almost thrown out his plan and dragged her right to the floor once he spotted her. The pink bling jeans were gone. The glittery T-shirts were tucked away, along with the sparkly sneakers. Tonight, she wore a lipstick-red dress that dared a man not to notice. With plunging cleavage and a skirt that twirled with every spin on the floor, those gorgeous, naked legs teased him with every turn. Her shoes were low heeled with a peekaboo toe and made strictly for dancing. He knew this because his own shoes had been custom made over a year ago. Her blonde hair whipped in the air, teasing her bare shoulders, practically begging him to fist all those silky strands in his hand and pull. Hard.

His dick wept, pressing against the ridge of his jeans. His breath was shallow, his muscles locked in anticipation of what was about to happen. For the first time, he was throwing rational logic away. He had one goal tonight and he wouldn't leave until it was achieved, no matter what the consequences.

Tonight, he was going to salsa dance with Charlotte Grayson.

Slowly, he dragged in a lungful of air. Steadied himself. Unbuttoned his cuffs and slowly rolled up his shirt sleeves. Undid the first two buttons of his shirt. Put his beer down on the ledge.

And went over to claim her.

* * * *

She was laughing as Gage masterfully led her into a tight spin. Pivoting on her heel, the room whirled around in blurred images until her gaze snagged on a figure walking toward her.

Charlie squinted, sure she was imagining things, until he stood before her. Leashed power radiated in waves, wrapping her within a snug circle of male demand. He nailed her with his stare, those sooty eyes seething with a raw emotion that drove the breath from her lungs. One blue-black curl fell across his forehead in disarray. He'd unbuttoned his shirt and rolled up his cuffs, exposing sinewy arms sprinkled with dark hair. "May I cut in?" His voice was formal, but his gravelly tone dripped with command. He never broke his gaze, lifting his hand and offering it to her.

In seconds, her skin prickled with goose bumps, and her nipples pushed against the thin jersey of her dress. She squeezed her thighs together, suddenly wet and aroused, her core throbbing with need. She blinked, staring at his outstretched hand in half fear, half fascination. What was happening? What was he doing? And why was he looking at her like a sleek panther who'd finally spotted his prey?

A chuckle drifted to her ears. Gage pressed her hand in Brady's. "Have fun, you two." He walked off without another glance, leaving them amidst grinding, sweaty bodies pressing against them from all sides.

"Brady, I don't think—"

With one swift movement, he pulled her against him, his hand pressed into the small of her back, forcing her hips to cradle his. Off balance, she automatically reached up to grab his shoulders. Her nails curled into those rock hard muscles, a groan rising to her lips. The pulsing sexuality of his body against hers short circuited her brain. Her swollen breasts rubbed against his chest, and his mouth stopped inches from hers. Carved lips curled at the corner in a touch of a smirk, but his eyes blazed with an intense sexuality she couldn't deny or escape. Her eyes widened at the evidence of his arousal, notched securely between her thighs.

"Are you dating Gage?" he demanded.

She blinked, completely disoriented at his direct question. "No. He has a partner named Tom."

Satisfaction carved out his features. "Good."

"I don't understand. You don't dance."

"I most certainly do dance."

"Why didn't you tell me?"

"You never asked." His gaze practically devoured her. His thumb slid a few inches lower, stopping at the curve of her ass. She shivered. "Dance with me, Charlotte."

This time, the sound of her full name caused a helpless shudder. Confusion swamped her. "Why?"

"Because I want to. And I think you do, too."

She stared back at him, tilting her chin upward with a hint of a challenge. "How do I know you can keep up?"

His lip quirked. Damn, he was smoking hot. That combination of arrogance and dark sensuality was wickedly tempting. It was as if a filter had been ripped off her vision, and she saw him in all of his masculine glory. This was crazy. She'd never been attracted to Brady Heart like this before. Had she?

He lowered his head and spoke against her ear, his breath a warm rush of air. "Take the chance. I'll give you what you want. What you need." He pulled back slightly, meeting her eyes. "You just have to say yes."

Standing still on the dance floor as couples whizzed by them, Charlie came to her decision. A slow smile curved her lips. She wouldn't make it easy for him, though. She intended to pull out all the stops and see if he had what it took. That was the only way she'd allow him to suddenly transcend from irritated coworker to dance partner. And maybe more.

"Yes."

The blare of the trumpet foreshadowed the challenge ahead. Never breaking his stare, he positioned his arms in the closed position, his strong fingers wrapped around hers. His hand burned a scorching imprint in the small of her back. Then he began to move.

The salsa was a dance very different from the tango—the dance of love. The tango relied on full body contact and was a dance of seduction unfurled in the center of the floor. The salsa was a tease, a flirtation, a promise of what could be. If she had one thing to bet on in life, it was that Brady Heart wouldn't know how to dance the salsa no matter how much he wanted to try.

She was so very wrong.

He was a master on the dance floor. She'd been used to dancing with Gage and Tom, and was comfortable with her own moves and their easy leads. They played at the salsa.

Brady owned it.

He moved with a speed and grace that took her breath away, leading with a command she'd never experienced. He gave her no choice but to follow, to bend to his will and the will of the salsa, until her body rose with its own demand and gave him what he wanted.

She spun away, launching into a short solo, whipping her hair and shaking her hips to the percussion beat, daring him to match her.

And he did, pulling her in, forcing her into a series of turns while he guided her with strong hands that took control. His red shoes flashed, his onyx eyes blazed, and each time she challenged him, he gave it all back, demanding more.

They danced until sweat dampened their skin and their muscles ached, and still the music pounded in a jungle beat, refusing to stop. The crowd around them disappeared to a distant blur and roar. She was caught up in another world of vast space and physical freedom.

He pushed her, punished her, broke her. With each step her will lessened, until she was a beautiful extension of his limbs, his lean muscles, his inward grace and leashed sensuality. He pushed her away, pulled her in, bent her so far back her hair brushed the floor, then pressed her so tight against his body, there was no separation between them as they became one.

Each time he brought her close, his hands ran over her body, stroked the bare skin of her arms, the curve of her spine, the hard tips of her breasts. Her body was lit from within with a fire that ravaged and burned her alive. It was a dance of seduction and intention, of lust and primitive need. And still, he never stopped, forcing her to meet each one of his steps and give her what he wanted.

Everything.

A whimper broke from her lips. He stopped, dragging her against his chest, his hand fisting in her tangled hair to tug hard, forcing her head back. He studied her face, a curse blistering in the air, and lowered his head. "Charlotte."

She waited. Then she rose up on her tiptoes, the decision already made.

His mouth took hers.

Like the dance itself, it was a fiery kiss that defied logic, a raw mating of tongues and teeth and want, stripped down to its basic form. Her head spun as she opened wider for his thrusting tongue, thrilling to the fingers digging into her scalp and his dominant kiss. His teeth nipped and his tongue dove deeper, swallowing her moan.

His taste swamped her with hunger, and she was mad for more, desperate to feel his lips on her naked skin and between her thighs, crazed to tear off his clothes and reveal every sleek, hard muscle.

He ripped his mouth away, dark eyes gleaming with fierce possession.

Time stopped. They stared at each other for endless moments, the world falling away and leaving them alone in a tunnel of raw emotion, burning hunger, and stunning silence.

His fingers lifted, grazing her swollen lips with the lightest of touches. "I've been wanting to do that for a long time," he murmured.

Her heart skidded, tripped, stopped. "About damn time."

That gorgeous mouth tipped in a smile. Before she could reach for him or say anything else, he dropped his hand and stepped back.

"Good night, Charlotte."

She watched in stunned silence as he left the dance floor and disappeared out the door, leaving her alone.

By the time she made her way back to Gage, she knew everything had changed.

She just didn't know what she was going to do about it.

Chapter Twelve

"Design must seduce, shape, and perhaps more importantly, evoke an emotional response."—April Greiman

When he walked through the door on Monday afternoon, she was waiting for him.

She hadn't slept in two nights. His image taunted her behind closed lids, tempting her with dirty, sex-filled scenes that made her body ache and yearn. He hadn't called or texted. Was he going to pretend nothing had happened between them? Did he believe they could just calmly go back to work without acknowledging what had happened on that dance floor?

Fine. If he could do it, she could too. She'd die before mentioning the kiss or the blistering connection or the way her skin burned when they touched. She'd pretend they'd never danced and melted into one another as if they were one. They could torture her and she'd refuse to admit there was anything else between them but work, friendship, and respect.

Her whole body prickled in recognition as he stopped behind her. She refused to glance back, concentrating on putting the finishes on her built-in cabinet.

"Hey, you're early," he said. "The cabinet looks amazing. Did you use the warm pine stain?"

Jerk.

She made sure her voice sounded light and airy. "Yes, the cedar was too red, and the kitchen needs a more open, casual feel."

His steps came closer. She practically felt his body heat pressing around her. "You distressed it, too."

"Yep. Again, this calls for a more worn look. What do you think?"

"Looks great. Didn't think you could pull it off, but once again, you managed to surprise me."

"Glad you can admit some things," she muttered, roughly sanding one ragged edge with a tad of violence.

"What'd you say?"

"Nothing. How was your weekend?" she asked.

She tried not to hold her breath. Had he seen Marissa Saturday night? Did he sleep with his potential wife after kissing her with wild abandon just a few nights before? She ground her teeth together and waited for his response.

"Kind of crappy. Went to my family's house for dinner. Had to do some work for Cal so that took up most of my time."

He could have texted her. A simple *How are you doing?* would have sufficed. She was on Twitter and knew he sometimes used the company account. Even a Facebook message would've been acceptable since she knew for sure they were friends.

"Cool."

She didn't say anything further. She concentrated on sanding, and practically felt him twitch with nerves behind her. Good. "How about you? Have a nice weekend?" he asked.

"It was great. Went out for drinks and dinner Saturday night." The lie sprung easily. Sure, there were drinks, but it was just a few glasses of wine alone in her apartment. Dinner had consisted of Gage and Tom taking pity on her and feeding her a three-course meal while they listened sympathetically to her complaints about Brady.

"Oh. Sounds nice."

Did his voice sound strained? Did he think she went on a date? She sanded the wood harder. "It was."

"Good." More silence. "Umm, I guess I'll finish the work in the bathroom."

"Great." She listened to his footsteps retreat, hating their ridiculously juvenile one-word conversation. Why did she suddenly feel like a teenager around him? And why did she care so much if he didn't want to talk about the kiss? Maybe it was just an experiment.

Now that he'd satisfied his curiosity, he wanted things to go back to normal.

She groaned when she saw the uneven edge on the cabinets she'd sanded down like a madwoman and swore to get her act together.

She hadn't mentioned the kiss.

Brady ripped at the last of the tile with a bit of violence. He was acting like a fucking idiot. He'd planned to call her over the weekend, but every time he picked up his damn phone, he choked. What was he going to say? *How's it going? Great kiss Thursday night? I've been thinking about you nonstop?*

Everything seemed juvenile, so he decided to just wait to see her in person. He intended to talk about the kiss right away, but she'd refused to turn around, like she was embarrassed to face him. Did she regret the kiss? Had it been an experiment and one she now wanted to forget? Or had she thought about it endlessly on loop like he had, unable to sleep?

He uttered a vicious curse word in Spanish. She could've gone on a date Saturday night and put the encounter out of her mind. If he mentioned it now, it might look like he was a damn puppy dog panting for some attention. Probably better to remain cool, focus on work, and see where the day took them.

As the hours passed, the tension between them grew, twisting so tight Brady felt like any moment they'd both snap. Jackson's absence made it worse. By the time dusk fell, they'd managed to avoid each other, exchange tight one-word sentences, and pretend everything was normal.

"Think you're ready to wrap up?" he asked. They faced each other across the living room. He tried not to linger too long on the ripe swell of her breasts contained in a T-shirt that declared, *Dream Big, Love Bigger* in baby blue sparkle. Her jeans were too tight, her lips were too tempting, and her eyes were too full of questions he wanted answers to.

"You can go without me. I'll see you tomorrow."

Her chilly tone caused the rubber band of tension to vibrate in warning. "I'll wait."

"I'm sure you have better things to do. People to see. Dates to go on. Sex to be had."

He jerked back. Studied her with a narrowed gaze. "What did you just say?" he asked softly.

She practically spit and growled like a pissed-off cat ready to pounce. "You heard me the first time. In fact, I've been thinking you don't need to be here anymore. Why don't you go off and do what you do best—find a neat little project to work on and a nice little woman to obey? 'Cause I'm done!"

And just like that, he snapped.

All of his doubts vanished, and he knew in that instant, she was just as crazed as he was. She hadn't forgotten their kiss. The memory was in her glittering hazel eyes, her shaking body, her tightly drawn tension. It was in the simmering heat pumping between them. It was in the tight tips of her nipples pressing desperately against her T-shirt, and her squeezed thighs and the madly beating pulse at the base of her neck.

Relief coursed through him. Now, at least he knew what to do.

Brady smiled real slow. Then crossed the room toward her.

* * * *

Charlie watched him close the distance between them. The entire day had been torture. She thought she could play the game, but she just couldn't. She hated thinking he didn't care about their kiss and refused to be one of those superchic, casual women who blew off any intimate encounter with jaded flourish.

Screw that.

"Why are you so mad, Charlotte?" he asked softly, getting closer and closer.

She stretched to full height, refusing to cower, and marched halfway to meet him. "Really? You have the nerve to ask me why I'm pissed off? We share this amazing, earth-shattering kiss in the middle of the dance floor, and then you walk out without another word? And when I think maybe you'll reach out over the weekend to acknowledge such a kiss, I get nothing. Well, let me tell you something, Brady Heart. I won't be used as some kind of Frankenstein experiment while you go off on real dates with Stepford women who are good enough to marry!"

"You think the kiss was that good, huh?"

Temper struck her. "You're an asshole!"

She launched for him in attack, but he caught her close, bending her backward, holding her tight in his embrace. She panted for breath, ready to pummel him, but stilled when she saw the raw truth glimmering in his dark eyes. "I can't stop thinking about that kiss either," he growled against her lips. "Can't stop thinking about you, like this, in my arms. Can't stop thinking about you being mine."

And then he kissed her, long and deep and hard. His tongue claimed her, holding her still beneath his demands. She curled closer to him, opened her mouth wider, and gave it all back to him full power. Finally, he broke away, his expression fierce with hunger.

She tried to speak, couldn't, then tried again. "That was unexpected."

His smile softened her heart. "Yes."

"How long have you had the hots for me?"

"Too long."

"I had no idea. Well, even after our almost kiss, I thought you didn't like me."

His brows drew together. His hands stroked her cheeks. "Not true. We may argue and I may disagree with your ideas, but there's a lot of things I like about you."

"Name them."

He lowered his head, his breath a warm rush in her ear. "I respect your drive and your focus. You have great creativity. You have a kind heart, and you make people around you feel good. You're funny. You're passionate. You know how to salsa. And your body is super hot."

A laugh hovered on her lips. "Did you just butcher the English language and say super?"

His teeth nibbled on her lobe, biting gently, then licking with his tongue. She shivered. "Sorry. I got caught up in the moment."

Her hands stroked the lean muscles of his back, the broad strength of his shoulders. "Were you jealous of Gage?"

"Yes. I've been fighting my attraction to you for a while. Besides the work conflict, you're ten years younger, plus I didn't think you were interested."

Her knees grew weak as he nibbled on her jaw, bit her lower lip, and kissed her again. "I never let myself go there. But I was always sneaking glances at your ass."

He chuckled. "Brat." He kissed her again. And again.

She leaned into him, hungry and desperate for more. He whispered her name.

"Yes?"

"Come home with me."

The words rang with primal need and a hunger that rocked her foundation. Charlie had learned life was a gift of chances and opportunities that were ripped away with too much hesitation. She'd never regret any decision of risk; her only regrets were the what ifs. Right now, logic had no place in her world. Right now, she needed him and refused to think about tomorrow.

"Yes."

He kissed her again, locked up, grabbed her hand, and led her out the door. She buckled herself into the cushy seat of his Mercedes. He pulled away from the curb, reached over, and entwined his fingers with hers.

They didn't speak. The sexual tension pulsed in the tight quarters of the car. The drive felt like forever, but in reality, it had only been fifteen minutes. He pulled down a quiet end street and into a circular driveway. He cut the engine, getting out of the car, and quickly led her up the pathway. Charlie got the impression of sweeping lines of brick and glass, of multi-level decks and huge windows caught in shadows. They reached the porch. He opened the door, punched in a code to his alarm, and shut it behind him.

Then in one swift movement, he picked her up high in his arms, spun her around, and slammed her against the door. His body pinned hers until each of her curves cushioned his hard muscles. His knee slowly pushed open her thighs while his hands cupped her ass, holding her still.

Her breath came in rapid pants. Her panties were so wet, they were useless as any type of barrier. The primitive gleam in his dark eyes declared his intention, but it was his words that made her practically reach orgasm right there, right then.

"I need to know how you like it," he whispered against her trembling lips. His thumbs caressed her jaw. "If you don't like rough,

I need to know now. Because I'm on the edge and I don't want to scare you."

Thrilled at his dark words, she parted her lips, running her tongue deliberately over the line of his mouth, then nipped with her teeth. "You couldn't scare me if you tried," she whispered back.

"Oh, the bad things I intend to do to you, Charlotte." He worked his knee higher, pressing against her throbbing pussy.

She half shut her eyes and fought the moan. "Then make them good, *Bolivar.*"

That did it. His grip tightened, and his breath dragged into his lungs with force. "What did you just call me?" he asked softly, in clear warning.

She nibbled at that delicious, firm mouth of his again. God, she was frantic to get him to kiss her, rip off her damn clothes, and fuck her properly. But she wasn't about to lose the first battle of the bedroom. "You heard me, Bolivar."

His low laugh promised retribution. "Have you ever begged, Charlotte? Really begged?"

Her tummy dropped. Her nipples were so hard they ached. "No."

"Oh, good. This is going to be fun."

He slammed his mouth over hers at the same time his knee pushed firmly in between her legs.

She cried out but he swallowed the sound whole. His tongue dove deep, dominating her mouth in delicious, wicked detail. She battled him back, tongues twisting, teeth gnashing, frantic for more of him to ease the yawning need devouring her. The barrier of her jeans was pure torture. His knee slowly rocked against her swollen folds, giving temporary relief, then ripping it away. Her clit pounded for more pressure, and she twisted in his arms, but he held her still, refusing to let her satisfy herself. He began rubbing his knee slowly back and forth, driving her out of her mind, until her fingers grabbed at the open collar of his shirt and ripped.

The buttons popped off and spilled to the floor. She tore at the fabric until his chest was bared, and her hands traced the gloriously hard muscles of his shoulders, his pecs, his rippled abs, scraping her nails along his hot skin.

He cursed. Yanked down the zipper of her jeans and tore them off. Fisted her T-shirt in one hand and guided it over her head, then threw the fabric to the ground. He growled in appreciation at the baby blue lace of her bra, but he divested her of it quickly, baring her breasts. He wasted no time, dipping his head to capture a hard nipple in his mouth. She arched against him at the same time his knee made torturous circles around her pounding clit, hazing her vision.

He sucked hard, plumping up her breast, flicking the tip back and forth before biting gently.

"Oh, God!"

"No, my name. What is it?"

"Bolivar." Damned if she was going to surrender this early on. She could hang on. Right?

He blew on her wet nipple. "Wrong answer."

His fingers slid under her baby blue panties and dove into her wet heat.

"Agh!" Her head banged against the door at the delicious pressure of his fingers deep in her core. His thumb played with her clit and he hit just the right spot to make her body explode with shivers, right on the verge of a shattering, mind-blowing orgasm. His teeth sunk into the tender curve of her neck while he added another finger, curling slightly and driving deeper. Lights shimmered in her vision, and her hips rolled with demand, seeking more, seeking…

"You want it? Ask me."

He was winning but she didn't care, not when she was so close to the best orgasm of her life. She rode his fingers in total abandon, digging her nails into his hips, head arched back.

"I want it. Now."

"Now, what?"

"Bastard. Now, please."

"God, you drive me fucking crazy. Yes. Come for me, Charlotte."

He bit her nipple, slammed his fingers into her dripping core, and flicked her clit.

She came. She screamed. She convulsed around his fingers, wet and throbbing, feeling so much pleasure it almost edged into pain. Instead of taking her down slow like most men did, he never stopped, pushing her further, rubbing her clit until she fell into a second orgasm whether she wanted to or not. Her legs clenched tight around his hips and she screamed again, awash in the sharp sensations attacking her from everywhere, flowing through her body like a river of hot lava.

She began to sag in his arms, and he scooped her up, carrying her up the stairs and entering a dark bedroom. He lay her down, the comforter soft and warm on her back, then quickly stripped off the rest of her clothes. Shadows slid and played over his figure. He unbuckled his belt and slid off his pants, then his underwear. Her gaze feasted on his gorgeous body. He stood with a sexy arrogance, hands on hips, feet apart, his large cock jutting out and making her mouth water.

Without thought, she crawled over the bed on all fours. "Let me touch you." She reached out and he slowly walked over, allowing her fingers to grip him, stroking from root to tip, catching the drops of moisture on the head. He groaned, stiffening more under her touch, and with a thrill of power, she dipped her head and took him in her mouth.

His taste was as delicious as his scent, musky, earthy, sexy. She licked and sucked, hollowing her cheeks and taking him to the back of her throat, humming slightly until he jerked in her mouth, and his fingers tangled in her hair, guiding her movements. Wild with need, she worked him until he ripped her away, cursing, and threw her back on the bed.

"I haven't even started and you already have me at the edge," he growled. "You're such a witch."

She pouted. "You made me lose control. Fair play, right?"

"Not in my bedroom."

"You chauvinistic, domineering, arrog-oh, God!"

She fell back on the pillow, gasping as his mouth hit her core. His broad shoulders kept her thighs wide apart, and he took his time tasting and exploring, his talented tongue using just the right amount of pressure on her clit, teasing her labia, bringing her straight to the edge again and keeping her there with a ruthless precision that made her want to weep and scream at the same time.

Her hips rolled in demand but he chained her to the bed, keeping his hands flat on her stomach and pinning her to the mattress. Her head thrashed. Her hands reached, her toes curled, and she did it again, dammit.

She begged.

He sucked hard on her clit and slammed three fingers inside her and she was coming again.

This time, he didn't wait. She heard a rip, he rolled on the condom, and with one quick plunge, he took her completely.

The burning, tight heat inside was almost too much. She whimpered, but he shushed her, pressing kisses to her swollen lips, stroking her breasts, gentling her for the invasion. Her body opened up, released, and he slid more fully inside. Rocking his hips, he kept up a teasing rhythm until the burning need was back in full force.

"Charlotte? Is this too much?"

She looked into his beautiful face. He gritted his teeth, and his jaw clenched with tension as he held himself back, waiting until she was ready. The graceful symmetry of his demand and patience, his dominance and gentleness, poured through her. She stroked his cheeks and wrapped her arms around his shoulders.

"Want more."

He pressed his forehead to hers and moved. Over and over, faster and faster, he fucked her more completely and fully than any man had before. His gaze locked on hers, never breaking the connection, drinking in every expression on her face. The wet slap of their bodies and panting breaths filled the silence, filled the darkness, and then the orgasm shredded through her, tossing her around the bed and wringing helpless cries from her lips.

He groaned and tightened his grip as he came right after, jerking his hips as he reached release. Bodies slick with sweat, the smell of sex ripe in the air, he held her close until she slumped into the mattress. "Be right back," he whispered. After a few moments, he climbed back into bed and cradled her against his chest. She didn't speak for a while, enjoying the tender strokes of his hand over her hair, gentle kisses pressed against her forehead. Completely boneless, deliriously giddy, a smile curved her lips as she lay in the darkness, enjoying the moment and the connection.

"You were right," she finally roused herself to say.

He stroked her hair. "About what?"

"You're a master at multiple orgasms."

He laughed, cuddling her closer, and her whole body sighed with pleasure. They fell into a comfortable, stretching silence for a while.

She stroked his chest, letting her thoughts guide her words. "What about Marissa?" she asked. "I know we weren't thinking this through. What are we doing, Brady?"

Her heart galloped as his muscles tightened. She hadn't planned to jump into bed with him, but now that it had happened, she realized she wanted more. More time with him. More time to see the man beneath the surface and everything he'd been hiding. Would he give them a chance or was this just a one-night stand?

"We never slept together," he said quietly. "And I won't be seeing her again, Charlotte."

She held her breath. "Why?"

"Because I don't just sleep with women and walk away the next day."

She rolled over, propping herself on her elbows. Her gaze narrowed. "Listen up, buddy. If you just want to see me again to soothe your good guy responsibility, forget it. I'm a big girl and I can handle it. We both wanted to have sex, and it was pretty damn awesome. I know we're very different, and we didn't plan on this for the long term. So, don't get all high and mighty and play the martyr because of guilt. Got it?"

"You are such a pain in the ass."

In one swift movement, he flipped her over to her back, pinning her wrists to the mattress. She blinked in astonishment at him. His sooty gaze held resolve, lust, and resignation. "You should know me better than that. I'm no damn martyr, and I'm honest. I happen to crave you, Charlotte, and it's not going away anytime soon. I don't intend to promise anything right now, except that I want to see you again. I enjoy your company, and I'd like to date. Is that acceptable?"

"That's acceptable." She paused. "Bolivar."

His grin was pure male and sent a delicious tide of shivers down her spine. "Did you just term the sex we had pretty awesome?"

Her lips twitched. "Yes."

"Have you ever had a spanking, Charlotte?"

Her eyes widened. "No!"

"Good. I'm going to enjoy this. A lot."

He flipped her over so she was on all fours. He pressed one hand to her back, forcing her down and leaving her ass high in the air. The other arm wrapped underneath her stomach, pinning her in place for every depraved, filthy, dirty act he wanted to do to her.

Oh. My. God. She was so frickin' turned on.

He seemed to know, chuckling low, teasing her with swipes of his finger through her wetness. He dropped kisses on the small of her back, moving downward, his tongue dancing over her sensitized skin. She trembled, aching for more, and when his teeth took a bite of her flesh, she moaned.

"You are so sexy," he murmured. "Baby, are you on birth control?"

"Yes."

"I can use another condom, but I'm clean and get tested regularly."

She pushed her hips back unconsciously toward his deliciously wicked mouth. "I am, too."

"No condom needed?"

"No." She wriggled her ass in abandon. "For months I've been begging you to talk more. Does the bedroom suddenly make you chatty?"

A burning sting hit her ass. She jerked, her breath hissing out of her lungs. Holy shit. "That hurt!"

He did it again on the other cheek. Then again. Oh, she didn't like this at all. She must not be into spanking and all that crap about it turning into pleasure was just that. Crap. She opened her mouth to tell him to stop right now, but then his fingers plunged into her pussy. Her swollen, wet folds clenched on him with fierceness, and suddenly, she was rollicking toward orgasm.

"Oh!"

His tone held a bite of laughter. "Like that, do you? God, you're soaked. You're so fucking sexy. I want to eat you alive."

He gave her a few more slaps. She tried to jerk away, but he kept her in place with his firm grip, forcing her to take it. Just like before, the stinging burn turned into a hot pleasure, until she was desperate with need.

"Brady."

Her voice broke on his name. He seemed to sense her raw urgency. Dragging her hips back, he kicked open her legs and thrust into her in one perfect, full stroke.

She buried her face in the pillow, swallowing her cries and

grunts. He fucked her hard, with merciless strokes that dominated and controlled, and she loved every moment. The climax dragged her under hard and fast, tossing her around, lighting her body with explosive pleasure.

She slumped on the mattress, boneless and exhausted. Barely able to move, she heard him get up and pad back with a damp washcloth. He cleaned her gently, pressing tender kisses over her skin, then tucked her under the covers. Never before had she felt so treasured and taken care of after sex. The light flicked back off. Then he climbed into bed, pulling her into his embrace. With his scent in her nostrils, and his warm, hard body cradling hers, Charlotte fell asleep with a smile on her lips.

Chapter Thirteen

"Creativity involves breaking out of established patterns in order to look at things in a different way."—Edward de Bono

"I have an idea."

Charlie set up the cans of paint in the kitchen and stared at the massive wall. Excitement nipped her nerves. She'd always dreamed of attacking a big-ass white canvas, and now she'd finally get to do it. She'd made some mock-ups of the image she wanted to create, but doing graffiti on such a large scale would be a challenge.

She glanced at Brady, who actually looked nervous. Those dark brows lowered in a frown, and he was studying the blank wall like it was a bomb and he was trying to disarm it. "What's your idea?" she asked, trying not to smile at his obvious doubt at her abilities.

"Wallpaper. We get some amazing wallpaper that makes the kitchen pop, and you don't have to ruin, er, paint the wall."

She shook her head. "This will be better than wallpaper. I deliberately went with wood and white cabinets, and underscaled the floors and countertops to balance out the artistic pop of a mural. It's going to blow your mind."

"I'm sure it will," he muttered.

She laughed out loud and rose, crossing the room to put her arms around him. Immediately he lost the worried edge, wrapping her in his embrace. Their bodies melded in perfect symmetry, and the scent of musk and spice rose to her nostrils. In seconds, she was hot, wet, and ready for him.

Two weeks.

Two weeks of nonstop, raw, carnal, hungry sex. It was something Charlie had never before experienced. They couldn't be in close quarters without needing to touch. The air seemed to crackle and come alive, as if it had been simmering the whole time, waiting to explode. So far, they'd spent almost every night together. She expected Brady to want to set up clear rules and boundaries—his entire persona was based around expectations and responsibilities for a relationship. Instead, when they ended work, they grabbed dinner together and headed back to either his house or her apartment, spending the entire evening naked and in bed.

Sheer heaven.

Deep down, she knew it couldn't last. Not like this. Eventually, they'd have to answer questions about what they were doing. But for a little longer, she embraced the moments with him, learning more and more each night. After endless orgasms, before sleep would claim them, they'd talk and share stories in the darkness, voices hushed, fingers entwined, slowly unveiling parts of themselves. The banter between them had also changed, softening to a lover's intimacy. Oh, they still argued with each other and differed with their opinions, but now the heat had a whole new meaning and was usually solved by ripping off their clothes the moment they were alone.

Unhealthy? Maybe.

Satisfying? Hell, yes.

"You're going to have to trust my vision on this one," she said, her hands slipping around to squeeze his ass. "Can you start work on the porch?"

"Yes. You're not going to paint girly type flowers, are you? 'Cause men use the kitchen too."

"Oh, really? I figured you'd peg the kitchen as the woman's domain. Doesn't Mr. Chauvinist expect his dinner on the table when he returns home from work?" she teased.

"Brat." His hand moved to her plump breast, tweaking her nipple through the fabric. Shocks of heat shot straight to her clit. He caught her expression and gave a very satisfied, male smile. "I have no problem with men cooking."

"Oh, really? Then what is it you truly demand from your woman?"

"What every man wants. A lady in the parlor. And in the bedroom a—"

"Don't you dare!" Shaking with outrage, she pressed her palm against his firm lips. "I swear, you were plucked straight from the fifties and sent here to live!"

His dark eyes twinkled with mischief. "I was going to say a bad girl."

She pursed her lips, still mad. "Ugh, that's awful and cliché."

"Oh, yeah? What do you want from your man? And don't give me all that fake stuff about a sense of humor, nice eyes, and to make you *happy*. Be honest."

The memory of their previous conversation rose up and mocked her. He wanted the truth? Fine. She'd give it to him and have a bit of fun along the way. She bit her lip, looked down, and plastered a guilty expression on her face. "Okay, you want the real truth? The ugly stuff I've never admitted because I felt like it was really wrong?"

Now he looked intrigued. "Definitely. Just let it rip. I can take it."

"I want him to have a big, well, you know."

He blinked. "Big?"

She licked her lips and tilted her head back, widened her eyes in pure innocence. "I need it BIG, Brady. Really, really big. It's kind of a fantasy for me."

Did he look worried? "How big are you talking?" His voice hitched just a tad.

"So big it not only shocks me, but breaks me," she whispered naughtily. Her hands coasted down his chest, tracing the line of the buckle of his jeans. "Bigger then you can ever imagine."

Oh, yeah, he looked a bit pale. "I see. Umm, do you have an actual measurement you were looking for, or is this just general?"

She shrugged. "Just the bigger the better. Boy, am I glad I finally admitted it. You're not upset, are you? I certainly don't want you to feel like you're not big enough for me."

The paleness was replaced with red dots on his cheeks. Giggles threatened to escape. She'd never seen him this thrown off before.

"No! Of course, not. I'm just, just glad you shared that with me."

"You can work on it. You know, if you want it to get bigger."

His mouth dropped open. "Excuse me?"

"Sometimes practice makes it grow."

"What?"

"Like random acts of kindness. Or charity work. Or just sacrificing for someone else in general," she rambled on, as if clueless to his growing horror. It took a few moments before her words really hit him, and then she knew she was in trouble.

"Charlotte. What part of the anatomy are you talking about?"

She smiled sweetly. "The heart, silly. I want a man with a big, big heart. What did you think I meant?"

His gaze narrowed and he made a move to reach for her. With a burst of laughter, she jumped out of his reach, backing up. "Oh, my, Bolivar. Was your mind in the gutter?"

"What time is Jackson coming today?"

The question took her by surprise. "Regular time. 3:30 pm."

"Good. Then we have plenty of time."

He stalked her with a slow, predatory grace. Her heart pounded as she looked down, making sure she wouldn't trip, and she managed to get into the living room. Uh, oh. He looked way too serious. "Umm, Brady, we have a lot of work to do. I was just kidding. A joke. Funny, right?"

"No."

She stumbled, regained her balance, and realized this was a very small house to elude a predator. "Don't make me pepper spray you again," she said desperately.

"Ah, thank you for the reminder. That's two punishments."

Was it wrong that her body practically wept with anticipation? She squeezed her thighs together, ignoring the wet achiness throbbing for relief. She was becoming a nympho and a spanking addict. Who would've thought her rigid, rational architect was so deliciously dirty in bed?

The thought hit her mind at the same time that her back hit the door.

Damn.

He wasted no time. In seconds, he laid his palms flat on the wood, caging her head. His hips pressed against hers, boldly dragging his erection over the notch in her thighs. Even through her jeans, the friction brought a moan to her lips. She gazed at his beautiful face, with his carved features, firm lips, strong, clean-shaven jaw. Those dark eyes seethed with lust but tangled with enough want and need to make her knees weak. That stray curl had once again escaped his neat style and lay over his forehead. Not able to help herself, she reached up and tucked it back, her hand stroking his rough cheek. Her breath whispered over his lips.

"You're beautiful," she whispered.

His eyes softened. Their gazes locked for endless seconds and something shifted between them. The lust became an aching tenderness that suddenly brought tears to her eyes. She battled her initial instinct to blink them back. Instead, she allowed him in, allowed him to see how he affected her. He sucked in a breath and his thumb dragged against her lips, his eyes delving deeper.

Her voice shook. "What's happening between us?"

She half expected him to step back, away from the sudden messy emotions surging between them. Instead, he smiled, dipping his head so his mouth was inches from her. "I don't know. You've ripped away my ideas and my plans and my control. You make me laugh, make me want to throttle you, fuck you, kiss you, take care of you. I thirst for you, Charlotte. Every damn day, I thirst for you."

The raw honesty of his words shook through her. She reached up on tiptoes, pressing her lips to his, the kiss so achingly tender the tears escaped and ran down her cheeks. He pulled her against him, wrapping her in tight, his tongue sliding between her lips to stroke and please. The kiss deepened, lengthened, stealing her breath and her heart and everything in between.

And that's the exact moment she tumbled head first into love with Bolivar Heart.

* * * *

Brady walked into the kitchen and took a deep breath. "I wanted to ask you a question."

"Hmm?"

She was up on the ladder, ass wriggling as she stretched to reach the top corner of the mural. He shook his head, fighting a laugh. She'd been obsessed with the painting, starting over three separate times and refusing to give up. Each day, he saw a bit more of the fuller picture, and though he was still doubtful, his intrigue was growing. The colors were muted earthy tones, reminding him of a Tuscan hillside. Mossy greens, muted golds, shaded burgundy. The blocks of graffiti were in 3D imagery that grabbed an onlooker, forcing them to give the wall their full attention. He might not be a fan of graffiti art, but he had to admit there was something compelling about the wall. Damned if he wasn't beginning to think she'd pull this off.

The real problem was her attention. The woman lived, ate, and breathed work, and as they neared the finish line, more of her focus revolved around perfecting every inch. The only way he was able to tempt her away from work was his body and the promise of endless orgasms.

He smothered a grin. He wasn't complaining. He'd never dated a woman so involved in her work. Most of his previous partners adjusted around his schedule and his career. He'd gotten used to making all the decisions, being the leader, and taking charge in all areas. Oh, he made sure he pleased every single one of them, both in and out of the bedroom. His satisfaction depended on the happiness of his partner, and he'd learned early being selfish brought disaster, especially to relationships.

But Charlie stomped on every single ideal he'd had for the woman he'd fall for.

She was vocal and had no issues stating exactly what she wanted and how she wanted it. Brady had never realized how much easier a relationship was when a woman played no games, or depended on him for happiness. From what they were eating for dinner, to how they renovated the house, to what DVD they wanted to watch, she negotiated the perfect balance of compromise. She was a giver, but also enjoyed taking, expressing her gratitude in such an honest way, it both refreshed and delighted him.

Both in and out of the bedroom.

She'd completely blown him away with her open hunger and sweet submission to every dirty, bossy, pleasurable act he wanted to commit. She owned it all on her terms, surrendering to her sensuality and bringing a whole new level to their lovemaking. He'd never been with a woman who could be so naturally submissive in bed, yet completely own it. There were no games between them, no pretending to be what they weren't, and in such acceptance, Brady felt more connected to her than any other woman before.

The more he learned about her, the more infatuated he became. He was changing, and he wasn't sure how to feel about it. Every time he took her in his arms, she chiseled off another part of him for keeps.

If things kept up, would he have anything of himself left? Was this a temporary affair that would eventually blow up and damage them both? He needed more answers, and there was one way to find out.

He tried to swallow back his nervousness. "Charlie? Are you listening? I need to ask you a question," he repeated.

"Sorry. Do you think brown is too dark?"

"No, I like it."

"Good. What's up?"

"I wanted to see if you'd like to come to dinner at my parents' on Sunday."

Her paintbrush froze midair. She swiveled around, pinning him with those expressive hazel eyes. "Wait. You want me to meet your parents?"

He shifted his weight, feeling ridiculously juvenile. "If you want to. I mean, I'd like you to but not if you're uncomfortable."

She broke into a joyous smile that made his heart stutter. "I'd love to have dinner with your family. I'm so excited to meet them. Will both your sisters be there?"

"Yes."

"Yay! I bet I'll get some serious dirt on you, dude."

He shook his head, grinning. "My sisters are well behaved, very unlike you. They won't share anything that may embarrass me."

She clucked her tongue and pointed the paintbrush at him. "You have no clue about women, do you?"

Her nose had a smudge of gold on the side. Her hair was covered by a ratty bandana. She wore old, baggy clothes, but her shirt was still carnation pink and her jeans had ridiculous pink bows at the ankles. She looked twelve years old and she was so damn adorable, he fought the urge to sweep her off the ladder and kiss her senseless. His throat tightened with emotion. What was she doing to him?

"I know more than you think I do. Shall I show you tonight?"

She threw back her head and laughed. "Yes, please. Oh, does your mom like flowers? Wine? What shall I bring? What should I wear? I can't wait!"

Sheer pleasure flowed through him. He rarely brought home a woman. It was nice to see her genuine enthusiasm to meet his family. She always made him feel good.

The door opened, and Jackson strode in. He was at the site about three times a week, and his mom was also a regular visitor. She'd stopped by to personally check up on where Jackson had been spending his time, and they'd connected immediately. She now joined them for their occasional Friday night pizza parties. Seeing the boy's enthusiasm with renovation filled Brady with pride.

"It's Friday!" he shouted, pumping his fist in the air. "Plus we have Monday off for some conference!"

"Nice," Brady said, grinning. They high-fived each other.

"Hi, Jackson!" Charlie called from the kitchen.

Jackson called a greeting back, but motioned Brady over with a worried look.

"What's up?" he asked the boy. "You okay?"

"Did you convince her to do the wallpaper yet?" he whispered. "'Cause the last time I saw that mural it was pretty bad."

He fought back a smile. "Nope. You know how stubborn she is. But she redid it again and it's getting better."

"Again? Man, why is she so stuck on graffiti? Just because it's in a black neighborhood doesn't mean we like graffiti in the kitchen!"

Brady couldn't help it. He burst into laughter.

"What are you guys laughing about?" Charlie yelled.

"None of your business," he yelled back. "Keep your attention on the mural, please."

He heard a series of mutters. He turned back to Jackson. "Let's give her support and see what happens. It is her house. Her decision."

Jackson sighed. "Yeah, I guess. Can I work with you on the porch so I don't have to watch? It makes me nervous."

"Yes. Let's go. Do some man work."

Jackson nodded and gave him a thumbs-up. They trudged out to begin sanding before staining the treated wood. At least they'd been able to save most of it and didn't have to rip the whole thing out.

Sure, it was a lot of manual labor, but he liked hanging out with Jackson, hearing about school and his friends, sometimes just sanding and being quiet with their own thoughts like men did. Somehow, some way, Jackson and Charlie had become part of the fabric of his daily life and changed him. They brought out the best in him.

They made him happy.

Brady refused to think about what would happen once the house was done.

Chapter Fourteen

"Discoveries are often made by not following instructions, by going off the main road, by trying the untried."—Frank Tyger

They sat cross-legged in a tangle of sheets, passing a bowl of cold pasta back and forth. "Now my illusions are completely shattered," she mumbled between bites. "Brady Heart eats in his bed. Who would've thought?"

"I don't allow anything with crumbs," he pointed out, popping a forkful of noodles in his mouth. "Nothing crunchy or melty."

"So, no chocolate. No chips. What about pancakes?"

"What about them?"

"Well, they don't have crumbs but they can get sticky with syrup."

"I like my pancakes without syrup so they're allowed. Thinking of making me breakfast in bed?"

She dropped her fork in the bowl. Her mouth fell open. "Not if you eat pancakes dry. You have got to be kidding. That has to be illegal."

He grinned. "You have no right to judge. I caught you slathering chunky peanut butter on your nonfat granola bar. That's a complete contradiction."

She stuck out her bottom lip. "I needed more protein."

"I checked the label. It already had 7 grams."

"Are you spying on me?"

He grinned wider and had the nerve to grab the last portion of the noodles. Even worse, he didn't look sorry. "Nope. Just an innocent bystander."

"I can't believe I'm dating someone who has no respect for maple syrup."

"I'm a good lay."

"Oh, that's right. You're forgiven."

They stared at each other, smiling, and her heart did a little skip. Oh, Lord, he made her giddy. She loved the way he surprised her just when he thought she had him pegged. He was a delicious contradiction of rebel and rules.

Her gaze swept the gorgeous bedroom. Decorated in rich woods and dark navy, it held both warmth and masculinity. The bed was king size, with an intricately scrolled headboard that Dalton had built him. Mahogany floors and furniture set off tasteful accents in navy blue and silver. The master bath could fit an entire family and was outfitted with a steam shower, jacuzzi tub, television, and a fireplace. If she were Brady, she'd never have the motivation to ever leave the bedroom.

His entire house held the same type of appeal—large, warm, and masculine. There were no feminine touches, but she once believed his home would've been more like a museum, impressive to look at but at the heart, cold and remote.

Instead, the intricate architecture, from its floating decks, multi-level staircase, and open loft, emanated an artful creativity she admired. He'd used different shades of wood to mix and match, from African walnut to teak, to rich red cedar. He seemed to have a thing for unique chairs—each room showed off various fabrics and shapes, startling an onlooker. His home clearly showed there were many layers underneath the surface to the man she'd fallen in love with. She only wished she had the guts to tell him how she felt and brave the fallout.

But she couldn't. Not yet. Not when things were still so fresh and new and perfect.

She comforted herself with the knowledge that he wanted her to meet his parents. If she wasn't important, he would have kept her away. Charlie refused to analyze his intentions and kept surrendering to the moment. It had worked beautifully so far.

"You never answered my question," she said. "What made you

want to be an architect?"

"When did you ask me that?"

She gave a long sigh. "That first time we drove to the Baker renovation property together. You were barely speaking to me at the time. Remember now?"

"Ah, yes. I do remember. But I think your question was phrased as 'Did you always want to be an architect?', and my response was a simple 'Yes.'"

"Damn, you're annoying."

"I try. Still want my answer?"

"Yes."

"I was always attracted to logistics. Balance. Numbers. My brain seemed to work well when I could grasp solid concepts and put them to use. But I also had a passion for architecture and drawing. My father suggested studying graphic design in college. I consider myself lucky that I knew exactly what I wanted to do early on."

"Dalton said you met Cal in college?"

"Were you asking Dalton questions about me?" he teased.

"Guilty as charged."

"Yes, I actually met Cal when we were in college together. His father was very generous to me and asked me to intern at the company. I loved working with everyone and it was a natural fit. After my degree, I became certified and immediately began working for Pierce Brothers. Eventually, I proved myself over the years and they offered me a partnership."

"I love that you embraced your father's suggestion. Teens are so rebellious. They'd fight their parents on anything."

He laughed. "My parents and I were always close. My father was strict, but we never had any issues, and I always felt like I was fairly treated. I had a good home life."

She squeezed his hand. "And you appreciated it. That's what makes you special."

He blinked in surprise, then gave her a lopsided smile. "Never really thought of it. But it's the same with you, Charlotte. The way you talk about your mom and growing up poor. You make no excuses. In fact, you make it sound like you were happy."

She shrugged. "I was. I had a great mom, and yeah, we had tough times but I always had her. And once she found a steady job, we managed to settle down and have a boring, normal life like I always dreamed about."

"Do you see your mom a lot?"

"Not as much as I want to. We lived in a small town in Pennsylvania. Our area wasn't the best to launch a design and renovation career. I came to visit my aunt and uncle and fell in love with Harrington. I just had a sense right away this was where I was meant to be. And I was right."

He leaned over and kissed her. She kissed him back, loving the leisurely stroke of his tongue, the gentle caress of his fingers trailing over her skin. The hunger was always there between them, burning bright, but as days passed, it grew into more tenderness, adding an extra layer that intensified the bond between them.

"Can I ask you another question?" she murmured against his lips.

"Anything."

"What is it about being an architect you love the most?"

He never hesitated. "Precision and numbers and control are all wonderful. But I'm really a planner of dreams. I help build a story, whether it be for an office or a house or an addition. That's the real value of my work, and that's why it never gets old."

Her heart stopped. God, she loved this man. The words hovered on her lips, caught up in a tide of emotion, but she kissed him again, and he pressed her slowly back into the mattress and then there was no more time for words.

* * * *

"I'm nervous," she blurted out. Her fingers clenched around the bottle of wine. He glanced over but he could barely see her from behind the huge bouquet of wildflowers she'd also brought.

"It's just dinner," he said patiently. "You're going to love my parents. And if you don't like them, let's set up a signal. If you kiss me, I'll know it's my cue to get us out of there."

"I'm not kissing you in front of your parents!"

"Okay. How about if you flash me your breasts, I'll make excuses and we'll leave."

"You are totally making fun of me."

"I am. We're here."

His family home always wrapped him up in the warmth and security of his childhood. It was a moderate-sized house, with dark shingled wood, a quirky tilted roof, and a cheery front lawn lined with bricks. His mother's vegetable garden took up the side lawn, and graceful weeping willows lined the property. There was no front porch—only a stoop—but the back deck was where everyone gathered for barbeques and parties. He'd offered many times to renovate his parents' home to their specifications, but his father refused, stating his mother hated to live in chaos with construction and strangers in her house.

He didn't knock, just led her through the door and headed straight to the kitchen. "Mama?"

"Brady!" She embraced him with open joy and enthusiasm, hugging him like it'd been months rather than two weeks since he'd seen her. "Who is this beautiful girl you've brought today?" she demanded, smiling at Charlie.

Why was his heart beating so madly? He felt like he was introducing his first girlfriend. "This is Charlotte. She likes to be called Charlie."

Charlie handed her the flowers, looking pleased at his mother's *oohs* and *ahs*, and hugged her back fully. His family was always touchy feely, preferring a hug over a handshake. Pride ruffled through him as he watched the embrace. He loved how Charlotte was so open and never exhibited distance.

"Thank you so much for inviting me to dinner," Charlotte said.

"If I had known you were coming, I would've made my special paella. This is the most wonderful surprise! I am so happy Brady finally brought a woman home."

Brady winced. Uh, oh. At first, he'd been surprised Charlie even agreed to join him for a Sunday dinner. He'd decided to avoid warning his family, afraid of the endless questions that would set off a barrage of phone calls. His sisters were nosy and his mother was panicked at the idea she wouldn't get grandchildren from him. He'd hoped to save them both the stress by just showing up with Charlie for a visit.

Probably not a great idea.

"Wait. You didn't tell your mother I was coming for dinner?"

He half closed his eyes. Yeah. The plan had definitely backfired. Now he had two women glaring at him with matching outraged expressions. "Sorry. I forgot."

"You forgot?" Charlie's voice went to a high pitch. "So, your sisters don't know I'm here, or your dad, and your poor mother didn't have time to make more food? Really, dude? Really?"

His mother watched her in fascination as he was scolded. He cleared his throat, struggling to get back on firm ground. "Mama loves company. Also loves surprises. Come on, let's meet the rest of the family."

He marched her firmly through the kitchen, ignoring her hushed accusations, and thrust in front of the family. "Hi, guys. Umm, this is Charlie. She's staying for dinner."

Silence descended. Everyone stared, not speaking, not moving, and the air thickened with anticipation.

Ah, crap. He should've warned them.

After all, it was the first time he'd brought a woman to meet his family in a long time.

A long, long time.

He'd screwed up and Charlie was going to kill him.

She was going to kill him.

She stared at the group of strangers in front of her. Even the children were gazing at her in astonishment, like she was an alien who'd flown in to visit from her spaceship. The three men were gathered around a big platter of various appetizers placed on a glass table in front of them. Two women, both dark haired and quite beautiful, stood in a corner with babies in their arms. One little boy with curly brown hair and his front teeth missing lay on the floor surrounded by toys. A little girl with pigtails and a pink dress clutched her doll close to her chest, frowning slightly in confusion.

Oh, my God. He hadn't told anyone she was coming to dinner, so no one was prepared. Was he crazy?

As the silence lengthened, Charlie swiped her damp palms over her dressy black slacks—which she'd picked out specifically for this occasion—and stepped forward. "It's such a pleasure to be here," she said in a bright tone. "Of course, I'm quite embarrassed Brady didn't tell you I was coming, but I hope you'll let me stay for dinner because everything smells delicious."

And just like that, the spell broke.

She was immediately enveloped in a swarm of family warmth. Brady's sisters—Cecilia and Sophia—chattered nonstop, holding out their babies—Armando and Angel—and introduced their husbands—Carlos and Michael. Brady's father, Bruno, hurried to pour her sangria, scolding his son for not telling them such a beautiful woman was coming to visit, and quickly escorted her into a comfy, overstuffed green chair.

The little girl—Alexa—jumped over, showing off her doll and peppering her with questions about how she met Uncle Brady and how did she get her hair to look so beautiful. They plied her with mini tacos, chips with guacamole, cheese and crackers, and crusty bread filled with spinach dip. Alexa sat on her lap, Cecilia and Sophia perched on the side of her armchair, and before the hour was up, Charlie had answered over a hundred questions and felt like she had a brand new family.

They were utterly, completely charming.

By the time dinner was called, she was already stuffed and had gulped down two sangrias, but then it started all over. She ate food she'd never been introduced to and became more amazed by his mother's cooking skills. Bowls filled with *menudo*—a thick, hearty soup with flavors of lime, red pepper chilis, and cilantro, danced with flavor in her mouth. Platters of steaming, tender pork shoulder, called *pernil*, paired with *arroz con gandules*, a simple, tasty rice with peas. The tortillas were stuffed with chunks of meat and seafood. The *mofongo*—a dish of fried mashed plantain with pork rinds— became her new obsession. The children sat in high chairs close to their mothers, babbling and eating happily as they were continuously fed tiny portions. Cecilia kept her baby perched on her lap, same as Sophia.

Charlie ate with enthusiasm, forcing herself way past her comfort zone, and finally fell back in her chair, dragging in deep breaths.

Cecilia laughed. "Ah, you're not used to the big Sunday dinners, huh? What do you usually cook for Brady?"

"Oh, I'm not a great cook," she admitted. "We've been

switching on and off, or try to manage a meal together. Two cooks are better than one, right?"

Sophia stared at her in surprise. "Brady cooks for you?"

Brady groaned. "I can cook, Sophia. I'm not helpless."

"I know, but you prefer not to. Then again, you're in the honeymoon phase. I'm sure things will settle down once you two get into a routine."

Charlie blinked. Had she heard correctly? A warning flashed in her brain but she ignored it. "Settle down?"

Cecilia waved her hand in the air. "Sure. Even Michael spoiled me rotten for the first few weeks. Then we settled down, and of course I took care of all the cooking. God knows, that would be a disaster if I gave up my kitchen to a man."

Michael tugged at his wife's hair playfully. "Hey, I made you breakfast in bed for Mother's Day."

"Burnt toast and pitted orange juice. But it was the thought that counts." They shared an intimate glance, obviously warm and loving. "How long have you two been seeing each other?"

Brady winked at her. Charlie relaxed a bit. "Well, we've been working on the house for a few months, but we officially started dating a few weeks ago."

Sophia sighed. "That's so romantic. Building a house together and falling in love. When do you think you want to get married?"

Married? She swallowed, noticing Brady stiffen in his chair, tight with tension. He tore his gaze from hers, focused on his plate, and shoved mouthfuls of food into his mouth. "Umm, we haven't really talked about that. We're just dating."

"But you want to get married, right, Charlie?" Cecilia asked with a pointed stare.

Heat rose to her cheeks. Thank God, Brady threw her a temporary lifeline. "We haven't discussed anything like that, Cecilia. Don't go scaring her."

Brady's mother cackled, offering more food to her sons-in-law. "Ah, nothing to be scared of. Marriage is a blessing of God and brings great joy with the right person. And once the babies come, you become queen. Mamas are well taken care of, and I know my Brady looks at his responsibilities to family very seriously."

Babies? She fumbled for her sangria and took a healthy swallow.

She would not freak out. She would not freak out. She would not…

Cecilia smiled at her like the subject was completely normal at her first family dinner. "I'm sure you want to enjoy a honeymoon period first, but I know how badly Brady wants kids. How many do you think you want?"

Brady groaned. "Cecilia, you're scaring her again."

Sophia frowned. "But you want babies, right, Charlie?"

Oh. My. God.

"Eventually," she squeaked.

"When do you think the house will be done?" Carlos asked.

"Umm, in a month or so. I'm very excited to flip the finished product. It's been taking up a lot of our time so we'll get a bit of a break."

"That's amazing," Sophia said. "I always wondered what it would be like to have a career, but there wasn't anything I felt passionate about. Except my children, of course." Her smile was brilliant. "They're a full-time job. Especially with the third on its way." She patted her stomach, which barely showed a bulge.

"Oh, congratulations," Charlie said. "That's such wonderful news!"

"Thank you, we're hoping for a girl this time around, but if not, we can always try again. Unless the third one finally does me in."

Carlos leaned over and pressed a kiss to his wife's cheek. "Ah, but you'd be bored without us," he teased.

She practically glowed with satisfaction. "I love it. Every part of it. And you will too, Charlie. Once you marry Brady and have his babies, you won't miss building houses."

Her fork dropped. "Wait a minute. Brady and I would never—"

Brady fell into a loud coughing fit, interrupting her and distracting everyone at the table. She stared at him, fuming, waiting for him to tell his family they didn't have that type of relationship and Charlie would never quit her career.

Instead, he chugged down water and quickly changed the subject. Before long, they were involved in a lively discussion about Carlos's job as a history professor. Charlie sipped her third sangria, watching the clear dynamics play out at the dinner table. The women murmured and chatted about the children, and the men talked about their careers and the challenges. When dinner ended, the men got up from the table and filed into the living room, leaving a table full of dishes, leftover food, and needy children.

"Where'd they go?" Charlie asked. "They aren't going to help clean up?"

The women stared at her like she'd sprouted horns, then burst into laughter. "Oh, now that would be a sight to see!" Cecilia said, getting up from her chair and grabbing a plate. "They play cards now."

"For how long?"

Sophia shrugged. "About an hour. We'll be done by then. But Charlie, you're our guest. Why don't you take a seat and chat with us while we clean up?"

She rose with the women, shaking her head. "Absolutely not. I need to work off some calories. I don't think I've ever eaten that much in my life. It was absolutely delicious."

His mother beamed. "Thank you. I can teach you how to make the paella and menudo. They are Brady's favorites."

She nodded, forcing a smile, but uneasiness flickered deep within. Was this what being with his family would be like? They were warm and gracious and wonderful, but would they actually expect her to give up her career? Dedicate her time to cooking and cleaning and raising kids while he owned the role of breadwinner? Did a relationship with Brady consist of becoming someone else? Or at least pretending to be?

She swallowed back her doubts and concentrated on helping the women. At one point, the two toddlers were wailing, but she engaged in a rousing game of peekaboo while they sat in their high chairs and soon had them giggling nonstop.

Brady's mother patted her shoulder. Charlie glanced up and noticed the dancing glint in her beautiful dark eyes. "I am so glad you came," she said quietly. "You are good for him. You make him happy."

"He makes me happy," she said simply. "But I don't want to mislead you. We're not, umm, we're not really serious. We're just dating."

The older woman cackled with merriment. "Brady doesn't bring someone home unless he's serious." She pointed to the two babies. "You will be a good daughter-in-law."

"Umm, I'm not—"

"Welcome to the family."

"But—"

She was pulled into a warm, loving embrace, quickly joined by Cecilia and Sophia, as if she'd just announced their engagement. And though her words sputtered in her throat, the denial hovering on her lips, a tide of yearning so intense crashed over her in waves, tempting her with an image she'd never believed could be a possibility.

The possibility of Brady loving her as she loved him. The possibility of his family becoming hers. The possibility of…more.

So Charlie said nothing and hugged them back.

Chapter Fifteen

"The most important part of design is finding all the issues to be resolved. The rest are details."—Soumeet Lanka

Brady wondered how certain silences could scream.

He glanced over and studied her face. After expressing how wonderful she thought his family was, she'd stopped talking. With each mile the Mercedes gobbled up, the tension grew between them. But not the usual hungry, sexual type he was used to.

No, this was the worst kind. The awkward kind. The kind he got after a bad date where he couldn't wait to flee the other person for a few hours to be alone.

He should've never invited her to dinner.

"Umm, would you mind if you dropped me off at my apartment tonight? I have some stuff to do."

He stiffened. It was the first time she was asking to spend a night apart from him. The searing pain caught him under the chin and knocked him back, but he gritted his teeth and kept his gaze on the road. "That's fine."

Back to silence.

Sweat broke out on his brow. Why had he done it? He'd always known his family thrived on tradition. It was the main reason he sought a woman who could offer him the type of lifestyle he'd grown up with. Charlie was a complete contradiction to everything he said he wanted. Marissa would've emerged from the visit steeped in happiness, ready to accept a ring on her finger and get pregnant on the honeymoon.

Charlie looked like she wanted to change her phone number, leave town, and pretend they'd never met.

He was such an idiot.

Anger ruffled his nerves. He grabbed onto it, liking the emotion so much better than the hurt threatening to overwhelm him. He'd never lied to her about what he wanted. He refused to apologize for his family dynamics because it worked and everyone was happy. When he came into the kitchen and found her wrapped in an embrace with his mother and sister, his throat had tightened and he'd barely been able to speak. The idea of Charlie being part of his life in such an intimate way made his heart soar. But when he caught her expression as he stepped forward, he'd crashed immediately.

She'd looked completely panicked.

Brady pulled up to her apartment building and waited.

"Thanks so much. I had a lovely evening. I'll see you tomorrow. Good night." She leaned over, pressing a kiss to his cheek, and started to get out of the car.

His fucking cheek.

No fucking way.

He flicked his wrist and cut the ignition. "I'll walk you up."

"Oh, you don't have to."

"I didn't ask."

He got out of the car and walked around. She seemed tempted to respond to his statement but decided to let it go. She slid the key in the lock, opening the door, but he gave her no opportunity to dismiss him again. He walked right inside and shut the door behind them.

His gaze swept over the room. They usually stayed at his house, but he was comfortable at her place. It was a standard issue, one-bedroom basic apartment, but she'd made it unique with her flair for design. Done in tones of pale pink, cream, and chocolate brown, the furniture was comfortable, with tons of throw pillows, shag rugs, and a rustic chandelier she'd created herself. The famous pizza box art she boasted about lined the walls of her sunny yellow kitchen, done in bright turquoise and pinks, adding a shock of color. Glass vases stuffed with various wildflowers sprouted from accents of mismatched wood shelving, homemade cabinetry, and a giant coffee table converted from a headboard. It was one of the most visually arresting, homey places he'd ever been.

"Umm, I really need to go to bed early, Brady." Her tone was the high, false one she used when she was nervous. "Can we talk tomorrow?"

"No." He put his hands on his hips and faced her. "I want to know one thing. How bad were you spooked?"

She jerked back. He waited, drinking in her expressions as she seemed to struggle with telling him the truth or giving him an excuse. Finally, she tilted her chin and met his gaze head on. "Very spooked."

"Better. I'll take honesty over bullshit any time. What spooked you?"

Temper flickered in her hazel eyes. "Don't try to bully me," she warned. "How dare you not even warn them I was coming! And what was that crap of you pretending to choke on your water to avoid telling them I'm not your baby-making machine?"

He took a step closer. "I wanted to buy some time, okay? My parents have always had a traditional marriage, and so do my sisters. They expect the same type of life for me. And don't you dare use that expression. My sisters are happy being homemakers and I refuse to allow you to judge them."

"I'm not judging them, you idiot! I adored them. You dare to think I have a problem about women choosing to do what makes them happy? 'Cause if you think that, you can march your ass right out of my apartment and don't come back."

"You certainly seemed freaked out."

"Because they didn't even stop to think I didn't want that type of life. I'm not them, Brady. I never pretended to be."

He stood in front of her, seething with a bunch of tangled emotions that made him roar like a pissed-off lion. "I never pretended to hide what my family is like or what type of woman fits with my lifestyle."

She breathed hard, cheeks flushed, fists clenched. Damn her. Why did she have to be so sexy and hot when she argued with him? Why was he so attracted to a difficult, bullheaded woman who'd choose career over love? "Is that what you want then? Because if you do, what the hell are you doing with me?"

"I don't know! I never planned on you. Never planned you'd

wreck me and make me want you so bad, I'd do anything to have you."

She gasped, pressing her fingers to her lips. The room hummed with electricity. Those hazel eyes burned with a raw emotion he'd never seen before she quickly banked the flames. "Even give up your ideals? Your detailed plans for the future? Because I will never be that woman. I will never want to cook and run a household and watch the children while you go out every day to live your dreams." Her voice broke. "It would destroy me."

The truth choked him with fear and need and pure confusion. What did he want? Could he give up his own dreams of a future with a wife who suited his needs? Or had he believed in something for so long, he never questioned the possibility of falling for someone else? Someone with different plans in life. Someone who made him hunger from his very soul and filled him with a peace he'd never experienced.

"I know it would," he ground out in the shattering silence. "I'd never ask that of you."

She wrapped her arms around her chest as if seeking comfort. He fought back the impulse to cross the room and pull her against him. "How can we keep going on like this?" she asked. "We fell into a sexual affair and it worked because we asked nothing else of the other. We lived day to day. But eventually, we were going to have to face the truth and decide what we both really want from each other."

"I'm not ready to give you up."

His stark admission fell between them and lay there, waiting for her answer. He couldn't bear the idea of losing her. Panic hit him from all directions, and he felt like a wild animal locked in a cage, desperate to move.

"During dinner, when your family assumed my career meant little to me, you never defended me. Never said what you wanted or that my choices were just as important as yours. Are you ready to tell your family our relationship will never be like theirs? That I'll never be a traditional wife?"

"Do you want children, Charlotte?"

He asked the question with nausea burning in his gut. His dream of a family was important. Could he possibly give that up for her?

"Yes."

His chest loosened and he let out a breath.

"But not now. Not for a few more years. I don't have a blueprint of my life like you do. I'm passionate about my career, and I want to build and renovate houses. I want to get married and have kids and have a beautiful house and a life full of chaos and joy. That's important to me. But not now. And I don't know when. Can you accept that?"

He studied the stubborn tilt to her jaw. The trembling of her lips. The too-wide hazel-colored eyes filled with fear and need and truth. That she'd never be enough for him. That eventually, he'd regret putting his own future on hold for a shot at something that might never work out. Was the risk just too great for both of them to take? He'd always longed for the type of family he was raised in, with solid roles for both sexes and a secure household. He'd never felt confused growing up or dismissed due to other obligations. He'd lived the happy, secure childhood he dreamed of for his own kids. Could he change his ideas for her? Be a different type of man? Or would their entire relationship be built on a lie?

He answered in the only way he could.

"I don't know."

Tears filled her eyes but she nodded, refusing to let them fall. "I understand. You have to go."

He knew then if he left, it would be all over. The light of day would rip them apart with rational conclusions and neat answers that made sense. He couldn't lose her like this. He wouldn't allow it.

"Brady—"

"You tell me that you don't want me." He closed the distance, reached out, and yanked her against him. "You tell me you don't want me to rip off your clothes and kiss you. Fuck you hard and deep until you come for me so many times, you forget why we shouldn't be together."

"Bastard! Why are you doing this now? I'm giving you what you want! I'm letting you leave nice and neat and tidy, just the way you like things!"

She pummeled his chest, but he knew it wasn't to get away. Her body was already burning, melting against him, her hips arching, her tight nipples evident from the sheer fabric of her shirt. He let her pound at him a few more times before snatching her wrists and pinning them behind her back. His other hand thrust into her hair and pulled hard, exposing her throat. His gaze raked over her face, taking in her parted bubble-gum lips, the hazy sheen of need in her eyes, and the pounding pulse at the base of her neck.

"I don't want you nice and neat, Charlotte," he growled, scraping his teeth down the vulnerable curve of her neck, sinking his teeth in the sensitive hollow of her shoulder. She shuddered. His dick strained against his jeans. "I want you dirty and needy. I want you begging. I want you so hot for me you'll do anything I demand."

"We can't make this about sex." Her voice was desperate, and he took advantage by running his tongue up her jaw, nibbling on her mouth, teasing her with tiny bites and licks that he knew would drive her crazy. Her low whimper was music to his ears.

"It's not about sex. It's about want. Need." His gaze crashed into hers. "It's about everything."

Refusing to wait another second, he slammed his mouth over hers, kissing her deep, his tongue thrusting over and over until she was a wild, writhing animal in his arms. Groaning, he lifted her up and carried her into the bedroom, laying her out on the comforter. He gave her no time to protest, quickly stripping her clothes off, then his, and joining her on the bed naked.

He was starved for her, and his slightly shaking hands showed her his desperation. Brady stroked every inch of her naked body, sliding over her lush breasts, teasing her tight pink nipples, tracing the gentle curves of her hips, the bare, swollen lips between her legs, all the way down her muscled thighs to her poppy-pink-colored toenails.

She cried his name, twisting under his touch, then arching to meet his tongue as he began to taste everything he'd touched. By the time he'd worked his way back up to her mouth, she was clinging, hooking her feet around his hips and arching for more.

"Damn you, Bolivar," she whispered against his mouth, eyes glassy with need. "Finish what you started."

A fierce rush of possessiveness seized him. This woman was his. She belonged to him, and they could fight, run, deny—nothing mattered in the end because she would always be his. He spread her thighs wider and reared up, poised at her dripping entrance.

"Yes, Charlotte."

Then plunged deep.

Buried to the hilt inside her, he practically roared with pride, feeling her swollen tissues clench around him, squeezing and holding him tight. She arched, shuddering, taking him all in, and then her head began to thrash side to side, her nails digging and tearing his skin with command.

He cursed and grasped her hips. He pulled all the way out, then slammed back inside her. Again. Again. Harder. Always harder.

She took it all, begged for more, and surrendered completely. Brady became a madman, completely enthralled with her smell and touch and feel, and it was never enough, so he bent forward to kiss her, his tongue mimicking his rolling, thrusting hips, demanding every part of her be open to him.

She screamed and thrashed and then his fingers found her hard clit and he rubbed gently, then harder and harder, and she came around his dick, drenching him with her climax, and he bit her neck as he shuddered and followed her over the edge.

He wondered if an orgasm could last hours because that's how it felt as the endless waves of intense pleasure rang through his body. She whispered his name in the dark, and he kissed her, feeling as if the earth had shattered and everything he'd once believed in was gone.

"What is it, baby?" he asked gently.

"I love you."

He pressed his forehead to hers, the joy exploding through him. "I love you, too."

"But I don't know if this will work."

It would. It had to.

Because he wasn't giving her up.

"Sleep now, Charlotte. We'll talk in the morning."

This time, she chose to obey. Soon, he heard the deep steady beat of her heart and her even breathing and he knew it had to be okay.

Chapter Sixteen

"Design is an opportunity to continue telling the story, not just to sum everything up."—Tate Linden

Charlotte tried to ignore the nerves jumping in her belly and concentrated on putting the last touches on her wall mural. It was all coming together. She had to finish sanding and staining the floors, paint the entire house, and deal with the property. She wasn't the best at landscaping, so she'd have to get someone to do some magic. And of course, the roof. Unfortunately, she was low on funds, even by saving on some other projects. She'd had to replace the refrigerator and stove, which came out higher than she thought after deciding to get a higher-level brand. The kitchen was the core of the house, and damned if she'd offer crappy appliances to a family. She'd have to wait a bit longer to save up for a roof, but she'd get there.

There was no reason Brady needed to be here to paint or work on floors. The main portion of the renovation was behind them, which meant his time was coming to an end.

And their time together.

She'd left before he woke, slipping out of bed around dawn.

She dragged in a breath, trying to ignore her aching heart when she thought of not being with Brady. Last night, she'd told him the truth. She was in love with him. What she hadn't expected was the words given back with a truth that devastated her. But she had already made her decision, and nothing would change her course.

Brady had always been truthful about his needs. He had a right to marry someone who would fit into his family. Someone who wanted kids quickly and embraced the role of housewife and mother. Someone happy without a career or the constant need to challenge her husband's leadership.

Someone who wasn't her.

They were opposites, a complete mismatch of wants, and furthering their relationship would only hurt them more when it ended.

She couldn't do it. Every day she fell deeper in love with the man. He spoke to her soul in a way she'd never experienced and transported her body to places she'd never gone. He was the man of her dreams, but because she loved him so much, she needed to let him go.

To find the woman who was meant for him.

"You did it."

She spun around at his familiar voice. He was looking at the mural, his expression full of respect and a touch of awe. Her voice was a bit creaky when she forced herself to speak. "You like it?"

He walked farther into the room, taking in the picture. She'd stuck with a Tuscan theme, but instead of gently rolling hills and distant colors, she'd created a pop-out graffiti effect of a house with a red tiled roof perched on the top of a tall hill. Earthy colors and splashes of burgundy contrasted with dots of stark white. It was a piece of art that seemed to pull a gaze and hold it; a mural that would never get boring and always be a conversation starter. The colors and image blended with the wood and white cabinets and gave the room a completely new look.

"Yes. But I'm not surprised. I should've learned to trust you from the beginning." He paused, then met her gaze. Her chest ached with need for him when she looked into his beautiful, dark eyes. Those lush lashes. Brown skin. Cleft chin. Wavy black hair. He was so gorgeous everything hurt just to look at him, because yesterday she had the right to touch him, kiss him, laugh with him.

"You could say the same with me," she said quietly. "I guess we changed each other's minds."

"I guess we did." He studied her for a while. "You left."

"Yes. I had to."

"Why?"

Her voice was steady but her heart was already in pieces. "Because I don't want to be with you anymore."

He jerked back, pain flickering over his face. She tamped down the need to go to him and soothe the hurt. Take her words back and say she'd do anything to make it work. But this was the only way and she had to follow her gut.

"Why?"

"I can't do this anymore. Please understand. You said it well. I'm ten years younger than you. I don't know yet what I want or when I even want to settle down. If we stay together, you could lose too much time looking for the woman you're meant to marry. A woman like your family wants."

"We can take it slow. Take more time. See what happens."

He winced, as if knowing his tone sounded desperate. Knowing he'd give up his pride to fight for her made her want to cry out, but she had to see it through. "Nothing will change. It's better this way. If we keep going, it'll get harder for me."

He took a few steps forward, then stopped. The scant distance between them yawned like a canyon and tore at her insides. His voice broke. "You said you love me."

This time, she couldn't hold back the tears that stung her eyes. "I do. But you were right. Sometimes, it's better to plan and follow your head so things don't get chaotic and end up destroying the very person you love. We want different things. It's time to be realistic and do what's right for both of us."

He spun around. Curses blistered the air. Her entire body trembled, waiting for him to come to the only conclusion left.

"We need to finish the house."

His flat tone ripped through her with sheer agony. She practically choked on her words. "I only have the floors and the paint job and minor landscaping."

"The roof needs to be replaced."

"I know, but it's not in my budget right now so I have to wait. Jackson can help me paint and do the floors. Gage said he has a guy who does good outside work for cheap. I'm almost there."

"You don't need me any longer."

She bit her lip, hard, to keep from crying out. God, how she needed him. Even now, she was practically shaking with the need to touch him, stroke back that unruly curl, smooth her palm over his forehead, and press her lips to his. He'd become a part of her in a few short months, and she had to relearn how to live without him.

She opened her mouth to respond, then fell silent. There was nothing else to say, and she was a few seconds from breaking down and begging him not to leave her.

"Very well. I'll see you back at the office."

And then she watched him walk out the door and out of her life.

* * * *

"Why aren't you at the house with Charlie?"

Brady glared at Cal and snarled his response. "Because the job is practically finished. Because she doesn't need me anymore. Because I'm trying to get this fucking plan together for Tristan, who didn't give me enough notice. Does that answer your question?"

Cal narrowed his gaze. "Yeah, it does. Get your ass in the conference room."

"I'm busy."

"Tough shit. Now."

He turned and Brady cursed at his back. All he wanted to do was concentrate on his damn job and he kept getting distracted. He was not in the mood to get into it with Cal, but he got out of the chair and marched into the conference room. Instead of sitting, he began to pace, needing to move. Lately, his skin felt stretched too tight over his body. He hadn't slept for over a week. He'd locked himself in the office until late, then went straight home and stayed there. He was either hopped up on caffeine or having too many beers at night.

He was fucking miserable.

Cal shut the door and took a seat at the head of the table. "What's going on?"

"I told you. Nothing. I'm busy. Charlie's at the end of her renovation. There's no danger—she's made friends with some of the neighbors and can take care of herself."

Cal rubbed his hand through his hair. "I'm missing something and you're gonna tell me. You've been a bastard this week. Sydney said you yelled at her regarding the new plans for Summit Avenue."

"They weren't ready to be filed."

"Syd showed me your handwritten note clearly telling her to file it."

"Fine, I made the mistake then. You wanna crucify me? Kick me off the board? Do whatever the hell you want—just leave me alone."

Cal's mouth dropped open as he stared in astonishment. "Holy shit, you slept with Charlie!"

Brady simmered with anger, treating his friend and partner to a nasty glare. "That's none of your business."

"Of course it is. You're like my brother."

The simple words were so truthful, the fight drained out of him, leaving him empty.

"Tell me what happened. You can talk to me."

In that moment, he realized he needed to dump the whole story to someone he trusted. So he did. He talked at length for a long time, confessing the ups and downs of the relationship and the final scene between them. When he was done, he felt a bit lighter. He forgot how Cal was able to listen and understand him as only a long-term best friend could. He'd been so careful to keep Charlie a secret, he'd stripped himself of an important support system in his life.

Cal tapped a finger on the mahogany table. "You know, Dalton bet me you had a secret crush on her but I told him he was crazy. Now all that animosity makes sense."

Brady sighed, dropping into the seat next to Cal. "Yeah. I wanted to deny the whole attraction because I knew it would change my life. And it did. Reminds me of Sydney and Tristan. They're so cold to each other, it's obvious something big is going on."

"They'll be forced to deal with their past sooner rather than later." Cal paused, cocking his head to study him. "You know, I see why you and Charlie ran into a problem. Would be so much easier to just stay in bed with our women, wouldn't it?"

Brady laughed. "Hell, yeah."

"I felt the same way when I first met Morgan. The problem doesn't seem to be how you feel about each other—that's the simple part. It's more about expectations of the future. Listen, Brady. I've known you a long time and you've always had a specific idea of the perfect woman in mind. You got thrown a curve ball. I guess you have to ask yourself, will this curve ball make your life better? Make you happier? Can you step away from what you *thought* your future would be and embrace what it could *actually* be? There's no guarantees with Charlie."

"I know and it's haunted me. I always wanted what I grew up around. Clear roles. Clear leadership. It seemed easy."

"Did you ever talk to your parents about their relationship?" Cal asked curiously. "As a child, you may have seen things a different way than what they did. Maybe you need to talk to them about Charlie."

Brady shook his head. "They adored her, but once they learn she's not going to be the traditional wife, they'll tell me to break it off. I know them."

"Sometimes people can surprise you. Remember when Morgan and I first got together? It took us a while to work things out, but I almost walked away when I found out she couldn't have children. My vision for my future included a bunch of kids and I didn't know if I would be okay accepting a different path."

"You're going to marry her this year. Do you have any regrets?"

His friend broke into a smile reflecting pure joy. "Not one. Not ever. Because I realized she's my person. My soul mate. She was my curve ball and it was the best thing that ever happened. She's my family, with you and my brothers and my dogs. And maybe we'll adopt or foster kids in the future. Your life can be anything you want it to be, Brady. As long as you're happy."

Brady stared at his friend for a long time, feeling something shifting inside.

Cal leaned over, clapping him on the shoulder. "Think about talking to your parents. In the meantime, I'm here for you. I don't want to step into your business, but I also want Charlie to know I'm here for her, too. Whatever you both decide, she's a part of the team, and we need to find a way to make things work."

"We will." Brady stood up. "There's one thing I need to do for her, though. The house is almost done but she can't afford a roof."

Cal frowned. "Are you kidding me? For everything she does in the company, I can send her some workers and get the roof done quickly. We'll give her a loan with no interest so she can pay it back whenever she wants."

Brady shook his head. "No, Cal. I'm already taking care of it. I need to. What she's done with this house is amazing. Her talent is something I rarely see—she sees things no one else can. I want to give her the damn roof, I just need the go-ahead to use some of your crew to schedule the work this week."

"Of course." He tilted his head, regarding him. "Did you ever think you'd be bored to tears with a traditional type woman? It's pretty rare we're able to find partners with the same passion for our work. I love working with Morgan. I know Dalton loves working with Raven. You share a special bond that many don't realize. Just a thought."

Cal walked away, leaving Brady with a lot to ponder.

Chapter Seventeen

"Great love and great achievements take great risk."—Dalai Lama

"Did you guys have a fight?"

Charlie turned toward the quiet voice. Jackson knelt on the floor, paintbrush in hand, concentrating on the back and forth strokes of his brush. But she knew immediately he was troubled. Dammit, she was making such a mess of things. Brady hadn't been here in the past week and it was affecting Jackson. She'd tried to explain Brady had other jobs to accomplish, but it was obvious Jackson didn't believe her. She realized lying to him was wrong. He deserved the truth.

Charlie put down her own brush and faced him. "No, we didn't have a fight. In fact, I think I'll always love him. He's kind and funny and fair. He's brilliant. And he was my friend."

Jackson stiffened, not moving. Then slowly, he turned and met her gaze. His wide dark eyes filled with wariness. "You loved him?" he asked quietly.

"Yes."

"Then why did he leave?"

She didn't want to have this conversation but it was important. Jackson faced his own problems on a daily basis. She knew he was being raised by a single mother. She had no idea about the relationship between him and his father, or if it even existed. He should know not every breakup was done to harm the other. Sometimes, it was just the opposite.

She sat cross-legged and blew out a breath. "I don't know if you're going to understand this completely, but I'm going to try. Brady and I started out not liking each other, as you probably saw from our fights."

A small grin curved his lips. "Yeah, you guys did like to fight a lot. But it was funny."

She smiled back. "Yeah, it kind of was. Then we became friends. Good friends. And then we began to fall in love the more time we spent together. But we realized as much as we cared about each other, we wanted different things to make us happy. We didn't want to end up hurting one another, Jackson. So, even though it completely sucks, and we're both sad, I want Brady to find the type of woman that will make him really, really happy."

Jackson scrunched up his nose. "Does he like redheads or something? 'Cause you could dye your hair."

She laughed. "Oh, I wish it was that easy. No. It's a lot more than that."

"My dad left because he didn't want a baby. Didn't want me." He uttered the words in defiance, his gaze hard. "I don't care though, 'cause we don't need him. One day, I'm going to do something great in life and he'll be sorry."

Her heart shattered, but she also knew she couldn't show her pain or sympathy. Jackson was an extraordinary boy, and he deserved his pride. "You're right," she said. "He's missing out on the best thing possible, and I feel sorry for him. Your mom gets all the good stuff. She got you."

Jackson nodded, his face softening. "Yeah. I'm gonna buy her a big house one day."

"Maybe you'll build her a house instead. You have talent. In fact, Pierce Brothers always takes on interns. I started as one. Maybe we can keep working together after this house is done."

His eyes widened. "You're going to get another house?"

"Hell, yeah. A ton more houses. And I kind of got used to you as an assistant, so maybe we'll talk to your mom and figure out a good schedule. If you're interested, of course."

"I'm interested."

They smiled at each other. "Then let's get back to work," she said, turning around so he wouldn't see the sting of tears in her eyes. "We'll order pizza tonight."

"Cool."

The knock at the door made her look up in surprise. "Wow, a real visitor. Let me check it out."

She peeked through the window and recognized Gary and Peter from the Pierce Brothers crew. Their truck was outside and a trailer was behind them with materials. She unbolted the deadbolt and greeted them. "What are you doing here, guys?"

Peter jerked a thumb toward his truck. "Ready to do the new roof."

Confusion swamped her. "What new roof?"

"This one. Was told to install the roof today for you and finish up the work tomorrow. Do you need us to come back another time?"

Oh, no. Caught between a rush of gratitude and pure stubborn pride that this was her project, she shook her head. "I think there's been a mistake," she said firmly. "I can't afford a new roof right now so this won't work. Sorry you had to come out here. I'll talk to Cal about it."

Gary grinned and thrust out a piece of paper. "Yeah, we were told you'd say that. Read this."

She opened up the note.

Charlotte,

I know you're going to try to send the guys back and say you don't want the roof because you need to do it yourself. I'm asking you to accept this as a present from me. For allowing me into your life, for changing me, for humbling me with your amazing talent and vision. I want to give you this roof so I will always carry a piece of you and Jackson in my heart, and in the house you allowed me to help renovate. Please.

Brady

Her throat tightened. She read the note again, almost sinking to her knees at the rippling waves of pain that crashed through her from his words. And she knew there was only one thing to do, for both of them.

She gave a nod. "Yes. Thank you so much. Today would be great."

"Cool, we'll get started."

She turned to Jackson, her eyes glittering. "We're getting our roof."

The boy let out a whoop, putting down his paintbrush. "Can I help? Or watch? Or carry supplies? Or do anything but paint?"

She laughed. "Go ahead. Tell Peter and Gary I vouched for your skills."

Jackson ran out of the house in excitement and Charlie hugged the note to her broken heart.

＊ ＊ ＊ ＊

"Son, are you okay? You're scaring us."

Brady looked at his parents, staring at him with slightly panicked expressions. He reached out and grabbed his mother's hands. "No, Mama. I'm sorry to scare you. I'm fine. I just wanted to talk to you both about a personal thing."

"Thank God." Her muscles relaxed, and she refocused on getting him to eat. "Have a snack. What else can I get you?"

His father smiled, staring lovingly at her. "*Querida*, let our son talk. He doesn't need anything right now."

His lips twitched. His mother lived to serve and loved every moment. It was part of the culture he'd grown up with, and his sisters had happily incorporated the qualities into their own marriages. "I want to talk to you about Charlotte."

His parents both lit up. His mother's voice filled with affection. "We loved her. So sweet and funny and smart. It was like she fit in perfectly here. And we've never seen you happier. You practically glowed in her presence!"

His father nodded. "Agreed. She's special. I've always hoped you'd find what your sisters had. Do you love her?"

"Yes, I love her. But we decided to break up."

His mother gasped. "What? How is this so? What happened?"

He laid his hands flat on the table and told them the truth. "I'm confused. Mama, Charlotte isn't like any of the other girls I've dated. She's different."

His father frowned. "Different how?"

"She's ten years younger."

"So what?" his mother burst out. "Cecilia is five years younger than Michael!"

"It's bigger than that. She's not the traditional wife I've always wanted."

His father's frown deepened. "Traditional how?"

Brady let out an irritated breath. "Like you and Mama. Like Cecelia and Sophia. She loves her job and never wants to quit her career. She has a passion for restoring houses and it's part of her soul—she could never leave it behind her to raise children and stay home. She won't be the type of wife to cook and clean and listen to me. Hell, I'd be lucky if she listens to me at all! She's stubborn and chaotic. She's the type to want her own checking account and challenge my every decision and probably drive me crazy. She won't be…easy. Nothing like your marriage or my sisters. You all have everything perfect."

He waited for his mother to jump from the table and tell him he was better off without this woman who was the model image of everything she was against for her son.

Instead, she threw back her head and burst into laughter.

He stared in astonishment as his father grinned, shaking his head.

"What's going on? What's so funny?"

His mother wiped her eyes and shared a look with his father. "Should I tell him or should you?"

"You, *querida*."

"My poor, sweet, confused boy. Your father and I certainly did not fall magically into these roles, and things are never perfect in a marriage. It is a living, breathing, fluid thing that changes as people change. We married very, very young because we were passionate about each other but I never thought my life would be about changing diapers and cooking dinners and meekly listening to your father's every command."

"You didn't?"

His father snorted. "Hell, no. We had two years where we traveled and partied. We fought a lot, we made up a lot, we figured out who we were. Then you were born and things changed."

"I was depressed at first," his mother admitted. "I used to work at a small retail store selling fashion and I loved it."

"You worked?"

"Of course. I gave it up when you came along but it wasn't easy for me. Your father and I fell into certain roles because they fit for us. He liked paying the bills, and I eventually loved staying home with you children. I began cooking with traditional Spanish dishes, and I found it satisfied a creativity inside of me."

"I got a promotion and the money was good, so there was no reason for your mother to go back to work. But do you honestly think I would've told her she wasn't able to work outside the home if that is what satisfied her soul?"

The room tilted. It was as if everything he'd ever believed suddenly changed, and he didn't know how to keep up. "Well, yeah. I thought you told Mom what to do!"

"I do," his father said in amusement. "Sometimes she listens. Sometimes she doesn't."

"Cecilia told me she'd like to go back to school once Angel gets older. Part time, of course. Sophia is happy being home with the kids and adores being involved with the mommy groups. She thrives. But I don't think Michael ever demanded she be a particular way. It's what works best for them."

"But—but everyone said they expected her to quit her job once the babies come."

His mother shrugged. "That was our expectations based on no solid information. But it's not yours. Not Charlie's. You run your own life and your own relationship. Is this why you broke up with Charlie? Because she wants to work?"

"Or does she not want children?" his father asked.

"No, she does, but not now."

His mother gave a relieved sigh. "Thank goodness. So, it's just a matter of timing for you two."

Brady rubbed his temples, trying to find his footing. All this time. All this worry about what his family expected from him. It had all been in his own head.

"Son, you have to ask yourself some important questions. If you actually want a wife who won't work and wants to raise children, that's a different story. Sometimes you can't change who you are inside," his father explained. "But if you're confused because you think we want you to have these things, you're wrong. We want you to be happy. To be passionately in love with a partner who satisfies you and makes you a better man. That's what marriage is about. Not who cooks or cleans or pays the bills."

And, suddenly, magically, his path was completely clear.

He didn't care about a traditional marriage, or who made money, or who cleaned or cooked. It had all been a distant mirage of perfection that didn't even matter. He craved a partner, a lover, a friend. He craved a woman who made him better.

He only wanted one thing to make him happy. One thing he'd been missing and searching for, over and over, believing it would fit his ideals and slide neatly into the perfectly square pegs of his life.

Charlotte Grayson.

The round peg. The one who shouldn't fit, but did. The one who rocked his body and his soul and his heart. The one he refused to live without for another minute.

"I have to go."

He stumbled from the chair, looking at his parents. "Thank you. I don't know if I say it often enough, but I love you. You've given me a life to treasure and showed me everything I need to know to be happy."

His mother covered her mouth with her hands, eyes shining with tears. "Good luck, my son. We love you, too."

His father nodded, and damned if Brady didn't spot the moisture in his father's eyes also.

Brady jumped into his Mercedes and sped off to claim the woman he loved.

Chapter Eighteen

"To design the future effectively, you must first let go of your past."—Charles J. Givens

"No! Fix it—don't list it, you idiot! Ah, what a waste of good money," she groaned through a mouthful of popcorn.

HGTV was so damn stressful.

She grabbed her wine, taking a few sips, and continued yelling at the stupid couple who was about to get into more debt for no reason other than they liked new.

The doorbell rang.

She stilled. Who could that be? She wasn't up for company tonight. After spending the day at the house finishing up details, she couldn't get over the present Brady had sent her. A new roof. So much better than anything she could've imagined. The man *got* her.

He just couldn't be with her.

She'd gotten so damn depressed she decided to order take-out, get in her old terrycloth pink Victoria's Secret robe with matching fuzzy slippers, and have a TV night. She'd eaten four slices of pizza, half a bag of potato chips, three chocolate chip cookies, and was about to demolish an entire bucket of popcorn. Her hair was stuck up in a Pebbles ponytail, her face was swollen from crying, and her mouth felt slick with grease.

Oh, no way in hell was she opening that door.

The bell rang again. Then again. Shoving the bucket off her lap, she marched over and peered through the slot.

Brady peered right back.

She jumped, slamming her palms over her mouth to muffle her cry. What was he doing here? The roof was his good-bye present, his final love letter; she knew it as well as he. Why would he go on torturing her with his presence? She was already dreading dealing with working with him day after day, but she'd grit her teeth and do it. But here, at her apartment, where they'd spent hours ripping off each other's clothes and playing sexy, naked, dirty games?

No.

He began to pound. "Charlotte, I know you're in there. I saw your eye. Open the door. I need to say something to you."

She looked down and groaned. "I can't. Now isn't a good time. Come back tomorrow."

His low laugh echoed through the door. "No, it has to be now. Right now."

"I was going to thank you for the roof."

"It's not about the roof. Open the door, now, or I swear, you're going to regret it."

"You can't talk to me like that! Demanding I open the door to my house after we broke up and you gifted me a roof? Who do you think you are? Go away."

"Open the door or I'll break it down."

"You wouldn't."

"Hell, yes, I would, and then your punishment will be worse when I spank your ass."

Her head spun with arousal and a blood-pumping anger. "You bastard! How dare you bring up sacred things we shared when we're not together anymore!" She turned the lock and flung open the door, glaring. "I don't know what games you're playing but I don't like them and I'm not the type of woman to let you walk all over her with a thank you so you better—oh!"

He jerked her forward and crushed his mouth to hers.

Her toes curled and her body sighed with bliss as his tongue dove deep to gather her taste, while he hitched her high up against his body to keep her still. She didn't fight, just wrapped her arms around him and kissed him back with all her own demands.

A long time later, he raised his head. "Pizza and popcorn?"

"I'm depressed."

He kicked the door shut and pressed a thumb over her lips. His dark eyes seethed with a naked hunger and something else. Something so wonderful she was terrified to hope. "You're so fucking beautiful," he murmured.

"What are you doing here?"

"Can't stay away from you any longer. I fucked up. I'm sorry."

Her lips trembled. "Oh, God, don't. 'Cause I can't send you away again. Please, go. Go and find someone who will make you happy, Brady. You deserve it."

"I do. And the only woman who will make me happy is you."

Misery shuddered through her. "I'm not good for you. Nothing's changed."

"Everything's changed. I realized I was being an asshole. I found the woman who owns my soul and I sent her away. But I figured it out, and I'm not leaving again. I love you."

"What about marriage and kids and your family?"

"I spoke with my parents. I was wrong, Charlotte. I cast them in a certain light and believed sticking to some roles would make my marriage perfect. The only thing that makes a marriage perfect is who you're with, and all I want is you. I want the woman who eats and breathes renovating houses and who's so cheap she makes cabinets out of windows. I want the woman who makes me laugh, makes me mad, and whose body I crave on a constant basis. That's you. And I don't give a crap about when or if we'll get married, or when and if we'll have kids. It can be two years, five years, or ten—I just want you for every single one of them."

The words were too much. The words were everything. But it wasn't just the words that made her realize what had changed. It was the open love and happiness carved in his features, the truth glinting in the depth of his sooty eyes. Somehow, some way, this man had fallen in love with her and wasn't going to let her go.

She jumped up, wrapping her limbs around him and kissing him. Her fingers twisted in his hair and she moaned with need as he walked her to the couch and they collapsed onto the cushions, still kissing.

"I love you and missed you and oh, God, you feel so good."

"You too," he growled, nipping at her neck.

"I look terrible," she moaned in between breaths.

"You look stunning. Even better once I get these clothes off."

She laughed as he tugged them off, and then they were naked and falling into each other like a beautiful poem where every word and stanza fit into the whole to achieve perfection. As he filled her completely, she cried his name. As she fell apart, he caught her. And as they lay sated in each other's arms, Charlie smiled. The future looked bright.

On their terms.

Epilogue

"I'm rich!" Charlie jumped up and down, clapping and dancing, while Brady shook his head and watched her. "I'm going to pocket $100,000! And not only that—Gage offered me the lot across the street for dirt cheap! The bank foreclosed and nobody wanted it and now it's all mine!"

She shook her hips, did a sexy wriggle, and tried to get him to dance with her. It was time to get her back to Tangos. "Congrats. I saw the new neighbors. Jackson seemed really excited to have a boy the same age move in."

"He's over the moon. And I'm so happy Cal liked the idea of doing a young internship program. I can't wait to have Jackson help me work on this house. This entire neighborhood will be transformed, slowly but surely—"

"House by house," he finished. She settled, and he gathered her close as they looked at the SOLD sign perched on the front lawn of their house. To him, it would always be their house, a reminder of their own personal love story played out plank by plank.

The couple who bought the house had two boys and they'd fallen in love with Charlie's renovation, offering full price. They were thrilled over the mural and the quirky touches that made the house special. It was as if it was made for them.

"Hey, I forgot to tell you Gage invited us over to dinner Friday night," she said. She tucked her arm around his hips and leaned in. "Figured we could go to Tangos afterward."

"Sounds good. Don't forget dinner at my parents' on Sunday."

"Already on my schedule. My place or yours tonight?"

She tilted her head up and gazed at him. His heart squeezed, and he fell deep into those hazel eyes that promised him the world and gave it to him on a daily basis. "Yours. I want you to show me how to make pizza box art tonight."

She giggled. "I can't wait to see this one. Just remember you can color outside the box."

"Don't be a brat, Charlotte."

"Don't be a hardass, Bolivar. Great art takes letting go."

"Great art takes discipline."

"Let's see whose is better. We'll let Cal, Dalton, and Tristan judge."

"Done. What does the winner get?" he demanded.

She whispered in his ear all the filthy, dirty ideas she had in mind, and in seconds, his jeans were way too tight.

"I can't wait."

She smiled up at him amidst the streaming rays of the sun.

"Me neither. For…everything."

Then she kissed him.

The End

* * * *

Also from 1001 Dark Nights and Jennifer Probst, discover Searching For Mine.

Sign up for the 1001 Dark Nights Newsletter
and be entered to win a Tiffany Key necklace.

There's a contest every month!

Go to www.1001DarkNights.com to subscribe.

As a bonus, all subscribers will receive a free
1001 Dark Nights story
The First Night
by Lexi Blake & M.J. Rose

Turn the page for a full list of the
1001 Dark Nights fabulous novellas...

Discover 1001 Dark Nights Collection Four

Go to www.1001DarkNights.com to subscribe

ROCK CHICK REAWAKENING by Kristen Ashley
A Rock Chick Novella

ADORING INK by Carrie Ann Ryan
A Montgomery Ink Novella

SWEET RIVALRY by K. Bromberg

SHADE'S LADY by Joanna Wylde
A Reapers MC Novella

RAZR by Larissa Ione
A Demonica Underworld Novella

ARRANGED by Lexi Blake
A Masters and Mercenaries Novella

TANGLED by Rebecca Zanetti
A Dark Protectors Novella

HOLD ME by J. Kenner
A Stark Ever After Novella

SOMEHOW, SOME WAY by Jennifer Probst
A Billionaire Builders Novella

TOO CLOSE TO CALL by Tessa Bailey
A Romancing the Clarksons Novella

HUNTED by Elisabeth Naughton
An Eternal Guardians Novella

EYES ON YOU by Laura Kaye
A Blasphemy Novella

BLADE by Alexandra Ivy/Laura Wright
A Bayou Heat Novella

DRAGON BURN by Donna Grant
A Dark Kings Novella

TRIPPED OUT by Lorelei James
A Blacktop Cowboys® Novella

STUD FINDER by Lauren Blakely

MIDNIGHT UNLEASHED by Lara Adrian
A Midnight Breed Novella

HALLOW BE THE HAUNT by Heather Graham
A Krewe of Hunters Novella

DIRTY FILTHY FIX by Laurelin Paige
A Fixed Novella

THE BED MATE by Kendall Ryan
A Room Mate Novella

NIGHT GAMES by CD Reiss
A Games Novella

NO RESERVATIONS by Kristen Proby
A Fusion Novella

DAWN OF SURRENDER by Liliana Hart
A MacKenzie Family Novella

Discover 1001 Dark Nights Collection One

Go to www.1001DarkNights.com to subscribe

FOREVER WICKED by Shayla Black
CRIMSON TWILIGHT by Heather Graham
CAPTURED IN SURRENDER by Liliana Hart
SILENT BITE: A SCANGUARDS WEDDING by Tina Folsom
DUNGEON GAMES by Lexi Blake
AZAGOTH by Larissa Ione
NEED YOU NOW by Lisa Renee Jones
SHOW ME, BABY by Cherise Sinclair
ROPED IN by Lorelei James
TEMPTED BY MIDNIGHT by Lara Adrian
THE FLAME by Christopher Rice
CARESS OF DARKNESS by Julie Kenner

Also from 1001 Dark Nights

TAME ME by J. Kenner

Discover 1001 Dark Nights Collection Two

Go to www.1001DarkNights.com to subscribe

WICKED WOLF by Carrie Ann Ryan
WHEN IRISH EYES ARE HAUNTING by Heather Graham
EASY WITH YOU by Kristen Proby
MASTER OF FREEDOM by Cherise Sinclair
CARESS OF PLEASURE by Julie Kenner
ADORED by Lexi Blake
HADES by Larissa Ione
RAVAGED by Elisabeth Naughton
DREAM OF YOU by Jennifer L. Armentrout
STRIPPED DOWN by Lorelei James
RAGE/KILLIAN by Alexandra Ivy/Laura Wright
DRAGON KING by Donna Grant
PURE WICKED by Shayla Black
HARD AS STEEL by Laura Kaye
STROKE OF MIDNIGHT by Lara Adrian
ALL HALLOWS EVE by Heather Graham
KISS THE FLAME by Christopher Rice
DARING HER LOVE by Melissa Foster
TEASED by Rebecca Zanetti
THE PROMISE OF SURRENDER by Liliana Hart

Also from 1001 Dark Nights

THE SURRENDER GATE By Christopher Rice
SERVICING THE TARGET By Cherise Sinclair

Discover 1001 Dark Nights Collection Three

Go to www.1001DarkNights.com to subscribe

HIDDEN INK by Carrie Ann Ryan
BLOOD ON THE BAYOU by Heather Graham
SEARCHING FOR MINE by Jennifer Probst
DANCE OF DESIRE by Christopher Rice
ROUGH RHYTHM by Tessa Bailey
DEVOTED by Lexi Blake
Z by Larissa Ione
FALLING UNDER YOU by Laurelin Paige
EASY FOR KEEPS by Kristen Proby
UNCHAINED by Elisabeth Naughton
HARD TO SERVE by Laura Kaye
DRAGON FEVER by Donna Grant
KAYDEN/SIMON by Alexandra Ivy/Laura Wright
STRUNG UP by Lorelei James
MIDNIGHT UNTAMED by Lara Adrian
TRICKED by Rebecca Zanetti
DIRTY WICKED by Shayla Black
THE ONLY ONE by Lauren Blakely
SWEET SURRENDER by Liliana Hart

About Jennifer Probst

Jennifer Probst is the *New York Times*, *USA Today*, and *Wall Street Journal* bestselling author of both sexy and erotic contemporary romance. She was thrilled her novel, *The Marriage Bargain*, was the #6 Bestselling Book on Amazon for 2012, and spent 26 weeks on the *New York Times*. Her work has been translated in over a dozen countries, sold over a million copies, and was dubbed a "romance phenomenon" by Kirkus Reviews. She makes her home in New York with her sons, husband, two rescue dogs, and a house that never seems to be clean. She loves hearing from all readers! Stop by her website at http://www.jenniferprobst.com for all her upcoming releases, news and street team information. Sign up for her newsletter at www.jenniferprobst.com/newsletter for a chance to win a gift card each month and receive exclusive material and giveaways.

Discover More Jennifer Probst

Searching for Mine
A Searching For Novella
By Jennifer Probst

The Ultimate Anti-Hero Meets His Match…

Connor Dunkle knows what he wants in a woman, and it's the three B's. Beauty. Body. Boobs. Other women need not apply. With his good looks and easygoing charm, he's used to getting what he wants—and who. Until he comes face to face with the one woman who's slowly making his life hell…and enjoying every moment…

Ella Blake is a single mom and a professor at the local Verily College who's climbed up the ranks the hard way. Her ten-year-old son is a constant challenge, and her students are driving her crazy—namely Connor Dunkle, who's failing her class and trying to charm his way into a better grade. Fuming at his chauvinistic tendencies, Ella teaches him the ultimate lesson by giving him a *special* project to help his grade. When sparks fly, neither of them are ready to face their true feelings, but will love teach them the ultimate lesson of all?

All or Nothing At All
The Billionaire Builders, Book 3
By Jennifer Probst
Coming July 25, 2017

HGTV's *Property Brothers* meets *The Marriage Bargain* in this third novel in the Billionaire Builders series, an all-new sexy contemporary romance from *New York Times* bestselling author Jennifer Probst.

* * * *

Chapter One

Sydney Greene rushed into the office of Pierce Brothers Construction, frantically calculating how she'd make up the twenty minutes she lost in morning madness. Her daughter, Becca, had insisted on wearing her hair in a French braid, then raced back to her closet to change twice before school. If she acted like this at six years old, what would happen when she reached high school? Sydney shuddered at the thought. Juggling her purse, laptop, and briefcase, she dug for the key. She was a bit of a control freak when it came to running the office where she'd worked since she was sixteen years old and liked to arrive before everyone else started. Order was the key to dealing with chaos. Her life had been such a series of sharp turns and fear-inducing hills, her soul was soothed in the one place she could not only control but thrive in. Her job. And finally, she was ready to take it to the next level. The office was quiet, immediately calming her. She dropped her stuff on her desk, then headed to the kitchen in a hunt for sanity.

Or, at least, some clarity. The kitchen was high-tech, from the stainless steel refrigerator to the cappuccino maker, soda machine, and various vending booths. With skilled motions, she quickly brewed the coffee, then grabbed her fav Muppets mug and filled it to the brim. Trying not to gulp the wicked-hot liquid, she sipped and breathed, bringing her focus to the upcoming presentation. After years of running Pierce Brothers as executive assistant and general office guru, she was about to make the pitch of a lifetime. It was time to take the next step and prove her worth. It was time to be promoted to CFO. And they had no idea it was coming. Nerves fluttered in her stomach, but she ignored them. She walked back into her office with her coffee, her Jimmy Choo high heels sinking into the plush carpet. She'd dressed to impress in her designer Donna Karan apple-green suit and even managed to pin up her crazed curls in a semblance of professionalism. Her black-framed glasses added a flair of style and seriousness. After grabbing her flash drive with her PowerPoint presentation loaded, she quickly set up the conference room with her handouts and laptop, then brought in a tray of pastries from Andrea's Bakery with a pitcher of water. Nothing wrong with a little bribing, especially when it involved sweets. She double-checked the room. Perfect. She was ready. She picked up her mug for another sip. She'd calculated this quarter's profits and could clearly show the margin of growth once she brought in this new— "Morning." She jerked at the deep, cultured voice breaking into her thoughts. Coffee splashed over the edge of her mug onto her jacket. Cursing, she swiveled her head, her gaze crashing into whiskey-colored eyes that were as familiar as her own beating heart. Familiar yet deadly, to both her past and her present. Why did he have to be the one who was here first? The man owned an inner alarm clock that detested lateness. She still hated the little leap of her heart when she was in his company, but it'd just become part of her routine. Kind of like eating and breathing. Anyone else would've brought a smile and a bit of chatter. But Tristan Pierce didn't talk to her. Not really. Oh, he lectured and demanded and judged, but he refused to actually have a conversation with her. Not that she cared. It was better for both of them to keep their distance. "You scared me," she accused. "Why don't you ever make any noise when you walk into a room?" Those carved lips twitched in the need to smile. Unfortunately, her presence rarely allowed the man to connect with any of his softer emotions, so he kept his expression grim. They'd been dancing around each other for over a year now, and still struggled with discomfort in each other's presence. Well, he experienced discomfort in the form of awkwardness. She experienced discomfort in the form of sexual torture. "I'll work on it." He gestured to the new brown stain on her clothes. "Need help?" "I got it." Her body wept at the thought of him touching her, even for a moment. Down, girl. She grabbed a napkin, dipped it in water, and dabbed at her suit jacket. "I didn't realize we were having a meeting today. I have some appointments."

"I rearranged your schedule. This is the only time that everyone was able to meet." "Another board meeting?" "Sort of." He didn't ask any other questions. He rarely did. She tried to ignore the masculine waves of energy that emanated from his figure. He'd always been the quiet one of his brothers, but he never needed words or noise to make his presence known. When he walked into a room, everyone noticed—men and women. He held a demeanor of competence and power in a whole different way from his brothers, Caleb and Dalton. As the middle child, he was a peacemaker and able to make decisions with a confident quickness most admired but never duplicated. His thoroughness was legendary. Tristan was able to see a problem at all angles and attack it with a single-minded intensity and level of control. He'd once brought that same talent to the bedroom, concentrating on wringing pleasure from her body with a thoroughness that ruined her for other lovers. She studied him from under heavy-lidded eyes. His suits were legendary—custom made with the best fabrics and cut that emphasized his powerful, lean body. Today he wore a charcoal-gray suit, a snowy-white shirt, and a vivid purple tie. Engraved gold cuff links. His shoes were polished to a high sheen and made of soft leather. He always reminded her of one of those jungle cats who prowled with litheness, amber eyes lit with intention, taking their time before deciding what to do with prey. His analytical mind was as drool worthy as his body. Hard, supple muscles balanced with a beautiful grace most men could never pull off. His hair was thick, perfectly groomed, and a deep reddish brown. His face was an artistry of elegance, from the sharp blade of his nose to his square jaw, full lips, and high cheekbones. Lush lashes set off eyes that practically glowed, darkening to an intensity that made a woman's heart beat madly. He was beauty incarnate, a feast for the senses a woman could never bore of while spending the rest of eternity studying every angle and curve and drowning in his cognac gaze. She'd once been that woman. Of course, that was centuries ago, before the ugliness between them sprouted from dark corners and swallowed them up whole. Didn't matter. She only dealt with Tristan for work now, though the past year had been more difficult, as she was forced to spend so much time in his presence. Those five years after he'd moved to New York and been away from Harrington were hard, but she'd finally grown up. Become a mother and made her own niche in life, rather than waiting for him to dictate her wants and needs. If only she weren't still attracted to the man. Already, the room surged with the innate connection between them. Some things never disappeared. They'd always had chemistry. Now it was just a matter of accepting it as fact and ignoring it. Most of the time she managed. "Let me settle in. We'll start in fifteen?" he asked. "Yes, that's fine." She turned away, discarding the napkin, and he left. She practically sagged in relief. Having him too close threw her off, and this morning she needed to be a poised, cool, confident professional.

Twenty minutes later, the team was assembled around the conference table. She tried to keep a smug smile from her face as they immediately attacked the tray of pastries, arguing good-naturedly over who got what and who saw what first. She'd decided on a sneak attack for her presentation. She knew these men well, and taking them by surprise would lower their defenses and allow them to really listen to her presentation without preliminary assumptions. The biggest problem working with Pierce Brothers for the past decade was also her greatest asset. She was like family. Unfortunately, this meant being treated like a little sister, which was also frustrating. She needed to convince them she was the best person for the job as CFO based on her business history. Not because of familial relations. "Who called this meeting?" Cal asked between bites of his favorite cinnamon bun. "It wasn't on my schedule originally." As the oldest brother of the crew, he was the most no nonsense, with a simple, rugged manner. He wore his usual uniform of old, ripped jeans, a white T-shirt, and work boots. His face was as rough as his appearance, from his hooked nose to his bushy brows and gunmetal-gray eyes, but he was always protective and held the wisest counsel she knew. He'd led the company along with his brothers when it was almost lost due to his father's will, but now they stood together, bonded once again by affection. "Not me." Dalton had his legs stretched out and propped up on the opposite-facing leather chair. She held back a sigh at the lack of professionalism. "I have no issues to discuss." As the youngest, he'd always been the wildest, and his woodworking talent was legendary. Stinging-blue eyes, long blond surfer-type hair, and an easy charm made women fall happily in line to warm his bed. Of course, now he was settled and in love with Raven. He'd grown and matured over the past year, and she had never seen him so happy. They both looked at Tristan, who shrugged. Elegantly, of course. "I was told my calendar was rearranged just for this meeting." The final member in the crew, not related by blood, was Brady. He lifted his hands in the air. "Nope. Have no idea what this is about." As the architect and longtime family friend, he'd carved his own niche for himself in the company. With his dark, Latin looks and commanding manner, he'd been essential to their success and easily held his own. Time to gain control of this meeting and do what she came for. "I did." All gazes turned and focused on her. She gave them a cool smile and flipped on her laptop so the first slide of her PowerPoint presentation flashed on the screen. After quickly distributing the stack of handouts, she stood at the head of the conference table. Already, she took in Tristan's fierce frown as he began flipping through the pages of her proposal. "What's this about, Syd?" Cal asked, finishing up his pastry. "As you know, I've been working at Pierce Brothers a long time. I started as file clerk, worked my way up to secretary, then executive assistant. I've been in charge of accounting, marketing, and managing the office staff." Cal cocked his head. "You want a raise. You don't need to hold a meeting for this. You deserve a pay bump."

"I don't want just a raise, Cal. I want to be promoted to CFO of Pierce Brothers. I want to be part of the board of directors." Dalton whistled. A grin curved his lips. "Man, this is gonna be good," he drawled, taking a bite of a simple jelly doughnut. Brady sat back in the seat, a thoughtful look on his face. Cal nodded, urging her to go on. She refused to glance over at Tristan. She didn't need any negative energy affecting her presentation. "I've been in charge of the accounts at Pierce Brothers for years, which goes beyond the standard accounts receivables and payables. Besides budgeting, I'm involved in negotiating with our local vendors for discounts and securing new jobs, and I have built solid relationships that keep productivity at increased levels. I've included a breakdown of the past quarter's profit margin." She clicked steadily on the slides, which were also included in the work sheets. "As Pierce Brothers has evolved, the workload has doubled, and all of you are consistently in the field. I've been able to fill in the gap by being more involved in the design aspect. Three months ago, I secured a new contract with Grey's Custom Flooring with a significant discount to our clients. I was able to do this because of my relationship with Anthony Moretti. Building up my main base of contacts keeps Pierce Brothers viable and able to keep offering unique materials to our clients." Cal tapped his pen against the desk. "I was impressed with Grey's. The quality is top-notch, and they've been easy to work with. You did a great job." She gave a slight nod. "Thank you. I'd like to show you how those savings affected our bottom line." She clicked steadily through the slides, breaking down each of her skills and leading up to the main event. It was time to bring it home. "I believe it's time to move forward. We're financially stable and ready to take on a bigger job with our redesigning and renovation projects." Tristan glanced up, frowning. This was the delicate part of negotiations. She was directly stepping into Tristan's territory, but it was time he realized what she could bring to the organization on her own. "I've been in talks with Adam Cushman. He's been very interested in securing some homes in the Harrington area and on the lookout for an opportunity. I believe he's finally found one." "Cushman?" Tristan narrowed his gaze. "He's the big developer in New York City. I worked with him briefly. How is it you know him well enough to be involved in such a conversation without my knowledge?" His voice was chilled, like one of those frosty mugs Raven used in her bar. She fought a shiver, determined not to let him intimidate her. Not anymore. "If you remember, you were in a bidding war with him for the property on Allerton. He came into the office one day, but no one was here, so I took the meeting. You ended up winning the property, but he kept in contact with me regarding future opportunities in Harrington. We both hold a similar vision on developing more family-friendly homes with touches of unique designs to court a solid middle-class-income bracket." "What properties is he interested in?" Tristan flicked out the demanding question with a touch of impatience. She gave a tight smile. "It's there in the proposal you're holding." She clicked to the next slide of her PowerPoint, sketching out a block of houses. "He'll be purchasing a total of eight houses on Bakery Street." Dalton stared at the screen, shaking his head. "Bakery? Those houses are in bad shape. Most of the tenants abandoned them, and no one's been interested in renovation for an entire block." "Exactly." She pushed the button for the next screen. "Adam has been able to purchase the entire lot and plans to renovate them all together, then flip them. This is the breakdown of approximate costs. We still need architectural proposals drawn up and design specifics discussed, but he's on board and wants Pierce Brothers to take the job." Tristan studied the papers in front of him like he was a lawyer about to take the bar exam. Brady scribbled notes in the margins, nodding. Dalton shot her a proud grin. It took everything not to smile back from his obvious admiration, but she kept her gaze focused on Cal. "Ambitious," he said slowly. "And brilliant. How'd you sell him Pierce?" "I want to use local suppliers for the entire project. I convinced Adam to go local instead of using the main manufacturing plants. We're concentrating on unique kitchen and bath features to appeal to middle income. Fenced-in yards, smaller-type decks, and appealing front porches for the lot." "Have you confirmed all our local suppliers will be on board with this?" Tristan demanded. "Many of them refuse to work with the bigwigs. They prefer local developers. Not city slickers, as they term them." "I've made initial contact and received definite interest.

I'd meet with them and get everything in writing before moving forward." "Well done," Cal murmured, still tapping his pen. "This is a huge job, Sydney. Do you have specifics?" She clicked to the next screen, which showed an organized calendar of tasks, assignments, and proposed time slots. "This is the working plan, but of course it will be tweaked as we discuss further." "I would've appreciated a heads-up before this meeting," Tristan clipped out. "I have another project in the works, and this will take up my calendar for the next several months. Why didn't Adam reach out to me before this?" She practically purred with satisfaction as she delivered the crushing words. "Because Adam wants me to lead this project. Not you." The men stared at her in slightly shocked silence. She smoothly continued her pitch. "Adam trusts me. He knows I'll retain his vision and be the main contact throughout the project. The only way he'll allow Pierce

Brothers the job is if I'm in charge. And the only way I'll agree to be in charge is if you promote me to CFO." Sydney snapped the laptop closed. The screen went dark. "I need something more. I deserve this opportunity. I know we'll need to hire another person to take over more office responsibilities, but I think Charlie may be interested. I know her primary love is doing renovation and rehab, but learning the business from the ground up intrigues her." Brady nodded. Charlie had come to Pierce Brothers as an intern, then slowly made her way to becoming indispensable for her skill in pulling apart houses and putting them back together. She and Brady experienced their own fireworks, beginning with intense dislike and moving to grudging respect and then something much more. Though they seemed like opposites, they fit together perfectly, and it was obvious how in love each was with the other. "Charlie actually mentioned she'd like to take on more work," he said. "It's definitely a possibility." "I have no problem hiring another person," Cal said. "Securing this project can be a big asset, especially for the future." Dalton grabbed another jelly doughnut. "I think it's amazing, Syd. Great presentation." "Thank you." Suddenly burning amber eyes pierced into hers. Tristan's lips pressed together in a thin line of disapproval. "You giving us an ultimatum?" She met his gaze head on, refusing to flinch. Refusing to back down. "I'm giving you a proposal. A smart one. And I'll be waiting for your decision. Adam wants to move quickly on this, so I'd like to be able to get back to him." "Fair enough." Cal rose to his feet. "Give us some time to discuss. We'll have an answer for you soon." She smiled. "I appreciate it." Scooping up her laptop and empty coffee mug, she walked out of the conference room with her head held high. She'd done it. Whatever happened next, she'd made her pitch and fought for what she deserved, for both her and Becca. After all these years in the background, it was finally her chance. She intended to take it.

On behalf of 1001 Dark Nights,
Liz Berry and M.J. Rose would like to thank ~

Steve Berry
Doug Scofield
Kim Guidroz
Jillian Stein
InkSlinger PR
Dan Slater
Asha Hossain
Chris Graham
Pamela Jamison
Fedora Chen
Kasi Alexander
Jessica Johns
Dylan Stockton
Richard Blake
BookTrib After Dark
and Simon Lipskar

49456705R00116

Made in the USA
San Bernardino, CA
25 May 2017